GUNS FOR GONZALEZ

Captain Slade Moran is tracking three army deserters who have stolen guns and supplies to sell to Mexican bandit, Gonzalez. Time is against Moran, and his situation is about to get even more complicated. The daughter of Gonzalez, fleeing her father's anger, is being pursued by Gonzalez's men, and by breakaway rebel Pedro Sanchez, who wants to use her as a bartering chip against her father. And when the bullets start flying, Captain Moran is right in the middle . . .

CORBA SUNMAN

GUNS FOR GONZALEZ

Complete and Unabridged

LINFORD
Leicester

First published in Great Britain in 2012 by
Robert Hale Limited
London

First Linford Edition
published 2014
by arrangement with
Robert Hale Limited
London

Copyright © 2012 by Corba Sunman

A catalogue record for this book is available
from the British Library.

ISBN 978–1–4448–1925–0

1

The heat was oppressive, like an extra blanket on a hot night. It drained Moran's vitality, especially as he travelled with the sun high in the noon position, when all animals and even rattlesnakes sought shade. But Captain Slade Moran, operating for the special investigation department of the Army of the Missouri, had, for two weeks, been on a hot trail in southwest Texas, hard on the heels of three army deserters who had killed the duty officer at Fort Broderick in the process of stealing two wagonloads of supplies, including five hundred new Springfield carbines plus three thousand cartridges. The wagons had headed south towards the Mexican border. Now, two weeks and many miles later, Moran was confident of catching up with the deserters. But he knew it was going to be a close run thing — the Mexican border was barely beyond the horizon.

He reined up to wipe sweat from his bronzed forehead as he peered at the featureless country to the south. Low, brushy hills lay ahead, bleak and barren in this unforgiving land that was arid and hostile to human life. The last hundred miles had been monotonously featureless, and he would be relieved to see different characteristics of landscape. He dismounted and stood motionless, peering around intently, alert for anything that could be considered unnatural in this godforsaken country. The wagon tracks showed that he was not far behind his quarry, but he needed to catch them before they entered Mexico, and he was prepared to die in the attempt to stop them in their tracks.

He was tall in a country of tall men, standing half an inch over six foot three. Broad shoulders and a narrow waist marked him as a man who was hard, lean and direct. His blue eyes were cold and impersonal under his down-pulled hat brim as he studied his surroundings for signs of movement. He was wearing a brown town suit, with a yellow neckerchief in deference to his cavalry origins. His headgear was a white cavalry campaign hat. He had a heavy cartridge belt buckled around his lean waist, the holster containing an Army Colt .45. A Springfield seven-shot repeating carbine — six shots in the magazine and one in the chamber — nestled in a leather saddleboot under his right leg, and he carried a .41 two-shot derringer as a backup in the right hand pocket of his jacket.

Moran checked his back trail before scanning the country ahead. If the deserters were aware of his presence then they would surely set an ambush for him before they reached the border. He noted the tracks heading on into the southwest while his mind picked over what he had learned of the thieves back at Fort Broderick.

Sergeant Avery, a veteran of twenty

years, had deserted from the fort with Corporal Hackett and Corporal Allen. All three had worked in the fort commissariat, and each had a blameless military record. But Major Bixby, their head of department, had been found stabbed to death in the armoury at the fort; supplies, weapons and ammunition were missing, and Avery, Hackett and Allen had gone absent without leave. Initially it was suspected that the three missing soldiers had set off in pursuit of the thieves, but Moran soon discovered the true situation, and had set out on their trail, his suspicions hardening as the trio headed unerringly for the Mexican border.

The robbery had been well organized, but it appeared that Major Bixby had surprised the men in the process of the job and paid with his life for being in the wrong place at the wrong time.

Moran was aware that a notorious Mexican bandit, Fernando Gonzalez, who pursued his illegal business both sides of the border, had acquired political leanings in addition to his long career of lawlessness and had let it be known that he was buying arms and supplies, and recruiting men with the intention of usurping the current Mexican government. Moran had no doubt that the deserters, planning to sell the stolen weapons across the border, had an arrangement with Gonzalez.

Moran, jerked from his musing by a faint movement in thick brush off to his left, was instantly alert for unnatural activity — birds rising suddenly or a jackrabbit running. He saw nothing, but his intent gaze suddenly picked out the head of a horse behind a large clump of mesquite. In the same instant he caught a glint of sunlight on metal as a weapon was lifted into the aim in the brush some feet from where the horse was standing.

Moran dived to his left, vacating his saddle as his outstretched right hand snatched at the stock of his carbine, which slid easily from its boot. He went down heavily in the brush, rolling to his left. A rifle fired in the same instant, its flat report hurling a series of diminishing echoes through the brooding silence. He heard a bullet cutting through the vegetation close to his head and rolled again to come to rest on his stomach, lifting his upper body on to his elbows. He raised his carbine and moved his head slightly to observe.

A puff of smoke was drifting away from the spot he had noted, and he squeezed off three quick shots, bracketing the small area. He eased to his left while the echoes were hammering, his narrowed eyes watching for signs of his target. A hatless figure arose quickly, moved through the brush a couple of yards, and then dropped back into cover. Moran fired again, without seeming to take aim. The figure jerked before vanishing into the brush. Moran knew he had scored a hit, and slid off to the left, keeping low.

One weapon had fired at him, he judged, and assumed that the other two thieves were still on the move with the wagons, following their original direction; intent on crossing the line into Mexico before pursuit could disrupt their plans. The man ahead had obviously been left to delay or kill anyone trailing them. Once across the border, they reckoned they would be safe. Moran grimaced at the thought and kept moving. He began to circle the deserter's position, staying low and moving fast.

The rifle that had ambushed Moran did not fire again, and an uneasy silence settled as the rolling gunshot echoes faded. Moran eased through thick brush, trying to move silently, and, when he was in a position to observe the area the rifleman had occupied, he took his carbine in his left hand and drew his Army Colt. He could see the brown horse, tethered to a manzanilla bush, swishing its tail at the swarm of flies pestering it. The man was invisible on the ground. Moran paused to check his surroundings, and his gaze was attracted by a tiny movement on a knoll to the south. He stiffened instantly, fully alert, aware that the action had not been made by an animal. He focused on the spot and watched it for some moments. The sun glared down, making observation difficult, but his eyes were shadowed by his hat brim, and presently he spotted the shape of a large hat just breaking the skyline.

It was a sombrero, with an up-turned brim and high crown. Moran frowned and continued to watch, but with one eye on the spot where the deserter had gone to ground. There was no movement and no sound from the surrounding brush. He watched intently, and as the tense minutes passed he picked out the shapes of three other men, all wearing hats out of Old Mexico. He wondered why they were taking pains to remain hidden and why they were north of the border.

But Mexican hats did not mean the wearers were Mexicans from south of the Rio Grande. Moran eased down out of sight and went on, aware that there was nothing the distant party could do to prevent him from getting his man. He eased forward cautiously. Sweat was running down his forehead. He reached the horse, which stamped and swished its tail. Moran paused, saw a US brand on the animal's rump, and nodded: an army mount. He noted tracks in the brush, followed them carefully, and came upon a man stretched out on his back with a splotch of blood showing on the chest of the dark blue shirt he was wearing.

The man was unconscious but groaning softly. Moran saw a discarded pistol, and, moving in to take it, thrust it in his belt behind his back. He placed his Springfield away from the man and closed in with his Colt steady in his right hand. The man was breathing laboriously, his chest rising and falling greatly, but he did not seem to be able to draw sufficient air into his lungs and was gasping spasmodically. His eyelids were flickering. He was dressed in range clothes. His pistol was an Army Colt.

Moran supposed he was one of the deserters. He holstered his pistol, examined the man, and decided that the wound was fatal.

'Can you hear me?' Moran spoke in a low tone. 'Who are you? What is your name? Why were you laying for me?'

The man's eyes flickered open and he looked up into Moran's face, but seemed unable to focus his gaze. His lips parted, and when he tried to speak a red dribble ran out of a corner of his mouth. He choked, blowing out a fine spray of blood. Moran waited a moment but the man settled down, slumping from within, his eyes closed.

Moran searched the man's pockets but found nothing. The man trembled. His left leg kicked convulsively. Then he gasped, subsided slowly, and remained inert. Moran felt for a pulse but found no movement. The man was dead. Sitting back on his heels, Moran studied the dead features. He had been given the name and a description of each of the deserters; this could be

Corporal Allen, who had been described as a redhead. There was a definite red glint to his hair, and even more in his face stubble. Moran picked up his carbine and eased to one knee. His immediate concern was to check on the four Mexicans.

There was no sign of them now. Moran studied the ground, but was unable to spot horses. He glanced over to where he had left his own horse and saw it standing motionless in the brush with only its head showing. He had field glasses in a saddle-bag, and needed them, but did not want to reveal his position for there could be several rifles pointing in his direction, just waiting for him to move. He waited patiently, sweat trickling down his face.

After a few tense, interminable moments his patience paid off. A rider appeared from behind a thick clump of brush and rode steadily to the right without looking around. The man was wearing a big black sombrero and had a serape draped over his shoulders. His

11

face was partially obscured by a large, drooping moustache. He was holding a rifle in his right hand, and sunlight glinted on brass cartridges in a bandolier draped across his chest from his right shoulder to the left side of his waist. He continued until he was lost to sight behind another clump of brush, where his cover was not so thick, and Moran caught a glimpse of the horse, which had been reined in.

Almost immediately, two more Mexicans rode into view from behind the same clump of brush and headed in the direction taken by the first rider. They were similarly attired, and carried rifles. Moran felt the first seeds of alarm springing into his mind and looked around quickly for the fourth man, fearing that his attention was being diverted by the three while the fourth was moving in to attack him.

A furtive sound in the brush close behind had him whirling around, his right thumb cocking his pistol. Before he could check it out, he heard hoofs crashing through the brush to his left and whirled again, dropping to one knee as he lifted his Colt. He saw a horse coming fast towards him. The rider was wearing a sombrero, and sunlight glinted on his upraised pistol. Moran threw himself sideways, flattened on to his belly, his gun hand swept up into the aim. The Mexican fired, and his slug cut through the brush within an inch of Moran's right ear.

Moran squeezed his trigger. The pistol kicked against the heel of his hand. The rider was within ten yards when the bullet smacked into his chest. The horse shied away and the Mexican pitched out of the saddle. He hit the ground only feet in front of Moran. The horse almost stepped on Moran, but jumped over him and continued through the brush, apparently heading back to where the other three Mexicans were positioned. Moran pushed himself to one knee, his gun covering the prostrate figure lying on its face in the brush.

The Mexican was dressed in drab brown — leather trousers and a charro jacket. Two bandoliers of bright rifle shells were crossed on his chest. His rifle lay several feet away from his inert body. Moran turned him over and saw blood spreading slowly across the front of his shirt. His eyes were staring sightlessly up at the blazing sun.

The echoes of the shot growled away into the distance as Moran bent over the man. He heard the crack of a furtive foot putting weight on a twig in the brush to his right and spun quickly, his deadly gun lifting. He halted his movement as his finger trembled on the trigger because the slender figure of a woman was rising up out of concealment, open hands extended towards him. Moran found himself looking at a Mexican girl.

'Where did you spring from?' He lowered his pistol.

'The man you have just killed is Paco Lamas,' she said in a quivering tone, 'and there are three other men with him. My father has sent them to take me back to Chihuahua.'

'I have seen the others,' Moran nodded, studying her. She would be no more than twenty years old, small, dark, and exceedingly beautiful, although at that moment her features were contorted by fear. She was wearing a red dress that was travel-stained and torn at the left shoulder. Her legs were bare; her feet encased in a pair of brown moccasins. She wore her black hair high on her head in a plaited coil.

'They were not after you,' she said. 'I do not think they would have harmed you if you had not drawn your gun.'

Moran glanced down at the dead Mexican. 'I had no choice but to shoot,' he declared. 'And this one sure was fixing to plug me.'

'And you have killed one of the gun-runners.'

Moran looked into her dark, inscrutable eyes. 'What do you know about gun-runners?' he countered.

'They gave me food last night, and

15

sheltered me. I left them when Paco and the others showed up, or there would have been shooting between them.'

'I'm hunting those gun-runners.' Moran frowned. 'They are army deserters, and stole weapons from an army fort. They murdered an officer.'

'They know you are tracking them.' She shrugged. 'I heard them talking in the night.'

'That one dropped back to ambush me.' Moran jerked a thumb at his would-be ambusher. 'I've been expecting a move like this for more than a week now. So why did you run away from home?'

'My father wants me to marry a man I do not love.' She spoke wistfully. 'I love another, but my father hates him. So I ran away.'

'I'm Captain Slade Moran,' he introduced. 'What's your name?'

'Rosita Gonzalez. My father is an important man in Mexico. He had only to snap his fingers and four of his men came to fetch me back. Can you help me, *señor*?'

'Anything I could do to help you will bring those other three Mexicans down on me,' Moran mused, 'and I'm up to my neck with the deserters. Ordinarily I would take a hand to help a lady in distress, but my duty is clear. I guess the only thing you can do is jump on Paco's horse and hightail it out of here. Where are you headed, anyway?'

'I have an aunt living on a rancho about twenty miles from here. She will take me in if I can reach her. But I will not be able to get away from the other three men sent by my father.'

'You're wasting time explaining,' Moran observed. 'Jump on that horse and hit the trail. If those Mexes try to pass me I'll hold them up to give you a chance.'

'Thank you, *señor*.' She turned, ran to where Paco's horse had halted, gathered up the reins, and sprang into the saddle. Bending low, she kicked the animal with her heels and set off to the north, vanishing quickly into the brush.

Moran heaved a sigh and looked around. He could see no sign of the three Mexicans. He checked his Colt before sliding it back into its holster. Silence pressed in around him. The two dead men were stark on the ground. He gazed at them while he thought of the two remaining deserters ahead, and a pang of impatience swelled in his breast. Then he heard the sound of horses coming towards him. He drew his gun, and waited for them to appear.

He turned suddenly and ran to his horse, thrust his carbine into its saddle boot, and swung into leather. The noise of the approaching horses grew louder. Moran cocked his Colt. The next instant two Mexicans emerged from the brush to his right, and the third crashed into view on his left. He ducked low in his saddle and triggered his gun when he heard a shot from one of the newcomers. Their intention was plain: they were going to kill him, if they could.

Moran aimed for the Mexican on the

left. The man was shooting fast, and not bothering to aim, being intent on drawing Moran's fire from his two companions. Not wanting to be caught in a cross-fire, Moran triggered two quick shots to his left. He heard the Mexican's first shot crackle over his head, and saw the man jerk away, then he turned his attention to the other two. Both were in the act of shooting at him. Moran kicked his feet free of his stirrups and dived sideways out of leather. He hit the ground on his left shoulder and twisted to bring his gun to bear. A bullet struck the ground near his left hand. He jerked up his Colt, swung it to line up on the nearest man, and fired. His teeth were clenched; eyes screwed up against the glaring sun.

The Mexican fell forward over the neck of his horse and the animal whirled away. At that instant, Moran felt the strike of a bullet in his right leg above the knee. The slug bored through the flesh of his lower thigh like a lightning flash, and pain flared through him as he lunged upright, wanting a clear shot at his man. The third Mexican was having trouble with his horse. Moran, half-deafened by the shooting, held his fire and covered the man, who brought his animal under control before looking up to find himself staring into the black muzzle of Moran's pistol. He paused for a fraction of a moment, then tossed his pistol to the ground and raised his hands.

'Get rid of all your weapons,' Moran rasped.

'You are making a big mistake, señor,' the man replied as he threw his rifle into the brush. He drew a long-bladed knife from a sheath beneath his shirt. His swarthy face was set in a hard expression and he was sweating profusely. His hard eyes held a dangerous glitter. 'We had no cause to fight with you. We would not look for trouble north of the border. We were after a runaway girl.'

'Out here?' Moran shook his head. 'You expect me to believe that? My guess is that you are bandits, and you

20

figured me for easy pickings. That guy over there came out of the brush, shooting at me without warning.' Moran pointed to the man Rosita had called Paco.

'Where is Paco's horse?'

'How in hell would I know? I shot him out of his saddle, and I guess the horse ran on. Now you'd better get out of here. I'm tracking some bad men. That one over there was waiting to ambush me, and there are two more like him up ahead with two wagons. Get away from here. Ride any direction but north or you'll have me breathing down your neck.'

'I would like to bury my friends.'

'Come back later and do it,' Moran advised. 'I'll know your face in future, so give me your name to go with it.'

'Aguilar — Tomas Aguilar. If we ever meet again, señor, you will learn all about me.'

'Get moving,' Moran rasped. 'I suggest you head west until I clear this area. I'm gonna stay here and watch you for a spell, and if I set eyes on you again I'll kill you.'

The Mexican turned his horse. He rode out slowly, increasing his speed as he drew out of gunshot range. Moran watched him until he disappeared into the brush a hundred yards to the west. He stripped his neckerchief from around his throat, shook it free of dust, and bound it tightly around his right leg just above the knee. Then he stepped up into his saddle, and when he rode out he left two dead men stiffening in the hot sunlight.

2

The army deserter, Sergeant Avery, twisted in his seat on the first of the two wagons and surveyed his back trail, uneasy because Corporal Allen, who had dropped behind to check for pursuit, was taking his own sweet time. Avery had sent Corporal Hackett to look for their absent companion, and he had heard shooting back there, followed by an ominous silence. Avery faced his front with a sigh. He had expected pursuit, and, having stuck his neck out, he was hoping nothing would go wrong with their scheme. But he wasn't happy with the way Rosita, the Mexican girl, had turned up out of the blue yesterday. He had expected to be met by a bunch of Fernando Gonzalez's men and relieved of the supplies before reaching the Rio Grande, not the bandit leader's daughter. The four Mexes who had shown up at sunup looking for the girl further complicated matters. Avery did not trust anyone from south of the border.

He had tied the horses pulling the second wagon to the rear of the wagon he was driving, and glanced around again to check as he continued. What in hell was Hackett doing? And where was Allen? Were they both dead?

Avery did not like the thought of being left alone. Hackett was the man who had handled the deal with the Mexicans, and knew everyone in the chain to Gonzalez. It would turn out to be a bad day if Hackett was gone. Avery's stomach muscles knotted at the thought. This was wild country, and the minute he crossed into Mexico he would be prey to every group of bandits that plagued the countryside like swarms of flies . . .

Meanwhile, Corporal Hackett, a short, powerful man in his early thirties, had no illusions as he rode steadily along their back trail. He was dressed in western garb in order to be indistinguishable from every other man riding the border. His blue eyes were narrowed and far-seeing, for he had heard shooting earlier and was expecting the worst. He had known that the army would not let them get away with the robbery, and the chances were that a troop of tough cavalrymen were now heading straight towards him. The thought made him veer away from the back trail and continue at some distance to one side. It would mean a hang rope if he were captured, for Major Bixby had been murdered, and Hackett had no intention of hanging for a crime he did not commit. He was already regretting taking part in the robbery at the fort.

He wondered about the four Mexicans who had shown up at the camp just after dawn. He had thought they were his contacts from across the border, but they had been after the Mexican girl. They had not mentioned the guns, but he did not trust them. Although he had been given safe conduct by Fernando Gonzalez, he knew enough about Mexicans not to trust them at any cost.

A horse whinnied off to his left and he whirled around, gun in hand. He could see nothing, and was about to dismount when Slade Moran called to him from a clump of mesquite.

'Drop your gun. I've got you covered.'

Hackett froze and released his gun. He turned his head slowly and saw a big man in a light brown store suit standing in the brush with a levelled pistol in his hand.

'What's this, a hold-up?' Hackett demanded.

'I'm Captain Moran of the army special investigation department, hunting three deserters from Fort Broderick who stole two wagonloads of supplies, weapons and ammunition. I have descriptions of the deserters, and I believe you to be one of them.'

'Not me,' Hackett replied. 'I've never been in the army.'

'You're riding an army horse,' Moran

observed. 'Dismount and put your hands up.'

Hackett hesitated, but Moran's gun was pointed unwaveringly at his chest. He stepped down from his saddle and raised his hands.

'You're making a big mistake,' he said. 'I'm riding with a freight train of two wagons that's heading into Mexico. We make regular runs across the border. When we heard shooting a while ago I slipped back to check it out because one of our crew was back there watching for trouble, and he hasn't showed up again.'

'What freight are you carrying?' Moran demanded.

'Mining equipment, provisions — everything connected with mining. We're heading for Chihuahua.'

'OK, so head back to the wagons. I'll check them out before I'll believe anything you tell me.'

'What about our man back here?' Hackett protested. 'I need to find him. He should have rejoined us before now.'

'Describe him,' said Moran.

Hackett did so, and Moran nodded.

'He's the man I killed,' he said. 'He shot at me without warning, and he fits the description I have of Corporal Allen, one of the deserters I'm trailing. You look like Corporal Hackett, so I'm arresting you on suspicion of being one of the men I want. Turn around and get moving. I expect to find Sergeant Avery with the wagons and everything that was stolen from Fort Broderick. Which one of you murdered Major Bixby?'

'I don't know anything about that,' Hackett replied.

'That's OK. Just get back in your saddle and take me to the wagons.'

Hackett swung into his saddle and turned his horse. He glanced at Moran, noted that the man was taking no chances, and headed back the way he had come. He was shocked by the turn of events. Allen was dead, and that left Avery and himself to handle the deal, but if they could not get the better of Moran then they were done for. They had expected pursuit — maybe a detail of cavalry that would make a sweep before giving up when they failed to find a trail to follow, but a single man on the trail, and an army officer at that, was a different proposition.

'Get moving,' Moran urged. 'And don't even think of trying to get the better of me.'

Hackett's spirits sank to zero. He rode as slowly as he could, hoping that Avery would be alert and could handle this formidable-looking military police-man. Moran stayed a few feet behind Hackett, his pistol in his right hand. Hackett could tell by Moran's manner that he was on top of the situation, and it looked likely that the run of luck they had enjoyed since leaving Fort Broder-ick had come to an end. The prospect of a rope around his neck was a chilling thought to Hackett as he rode reluc-tantly back the way he had come.

★　★　★

Avery drove the lead wagon, urging the team incessantly to make better time; anxious now because Hackett should have returned, his non-appearance indicating that trouble had befallen him. Avery glanced over his shoulder every few seconds, but saw nothing along his back trail, which worried him more than the sight of organized pursuit would have done.

When he glimpsed movement ahead, where he was not expecting to see any, he pulled his gun and cocked it, his nerves leaping. A rider appeared out of the brush as if he had been waiting for the right moment to announce his presence. Avery narrowed his blue eyes when he saw a Mexican astride a powerful black stallion, and his finger trembled on his trigger, for he had no friends in this part of the world where every man was a potential enemy.

'Did I startle you?' The Mexican spoke in English, and he looked a cut above the average bandit who haunted the border. He was young, in his twenties, and well dressed. His black sombrero, ornamented with a silver band, was pushed back off his forehead, revealing black curly hair. His dark, inscrutable gaze was unblinking. He wore a blouse of pale blue silk with a yellow serape encircling his lean waist, the end of which created a splash of colour against his blue woollen pants. The black butt of a pistol showed at his waist, where it nestled under the sarape.

'You shouldn't sneak up on a man in this neck of the woods,' Avery rasped. 'That's the easy way to get shot. Are you riding alone or are there more of you?'

'I am Alfredo Gomez,' said the Mexican, 'and I am looking for the girl I hope to marry — Señorita Rosita Gonzalez. I found her horse dead just this side of the border.'

'A Mexican girl came into our camp last night,' Avery informed him. 'She told us she was running from four Mexicans who wanted to take her back to her father. We fed her and gave her a blanket, and she was gone before sunup. Four Mexicans rode in later asking after her. As I remember, she said her name was Rosita Gonzalez.'

'In which direction did she ride, señor?'

'Like I said, she was gone when we got up.' Avery grimaced. 'I couldn't say which way she went. She didn't have a horse. She walked into our camp, and left the same way.'

'Those four men must have set her afoot,' Gomez mused. 'They were sent by her father to fetch her back home.'

'They rode off in that direction.' Avery twisted in his saddle and pointed along his back trail. 'I reckon they must have caught up with her by now. I did hear shooting back there some time ago. I sent a man to check it out but he hasn't come back.'

'That does not sound good.' Gomez reined his horse away and rode off in the direction Avery had indicated. He glanced into Avery's eyes in passing. 'Thank you for the information. You will have a dangerous trip when you cross the border. There are bandits waiting to rob you.'

'We have a safe conduct from Fernando Gonzalez,' Avery responded.

'He has big trouble at the moment because there is a difference of opinion between him and his top men. Some of his gang have broken away, and are led by Pedro Sanchez — they are the ones who will trouble you, *señor*.'

Avery touched the brim of his Stetson in acknowledgement and Gomez rode on. When the Mexican had disappeared in the brush, Avery shook his head. He applied the brake and jumped down from the wagon. The news was daunting. He was alone now, and would have little chance after crossing the Big Muddy; he would be murdered and the wagons stolen. He looked around. There was nothing but brush and silence, and suddenly he felt very alone. He had always been of the opinion that at least half a dozen men would be needed to get the supplies through to Gonzalez, but in view of this latest intelligence, it would probably take an army to make a success of the crooked venture. He decided to wait two hours in the hope that Hackett would return, but if the man did not show up then a change of plan would have to be considered.

Moran gave Hackett no opportunity of escaping. He stayed well out of arm's length and kept his pistol ready in his hand. The deserter rode sullenly, his eyes never still as he watched for a chance of reversing their roles. When he began to slow his mount, Moran called to him sharply, and Hackett clenched his teeth and went on, hoping that Avery would not be taken by surprise. Their only chance would be to overcome Moran.

Alfredo Gomez spotted Hackett before he was seen by Moran, and the Mexican approached openly, smiling a welcome. He lifted his empty right hand in a friendly gesture when he saw Moran's pistol swinging to cover him.

'I have spoken to the man with the

wagons,' he called. 'I am looking for Rosita Gonzalez, and learned that she came in this direction, with four men tracking her.'

'I saw her earlier,' Moran told him. 'She was in trouble with those four men. She said they had been sent by her father to take her back to him. They weren't friendly. I had to defend myself when they tried to kill me.'

'Are they dead, señor?'

'One surrendered. I sent him off to the west. The other three are back along the trail, stretched out ready for burial.'

'I am in your debt, señor,' said Gomez. 'Do you know in which direction Rosita headed? She will marry me when I can get her safely away from her father.'

'I sent her off on one of the spare horses. She was trying to get to an aunt who lives around here some place. She headed north.'

'Ah! I know her destination. She will be safe with her aunt. You have relieved me of a great deal of worry, señor.'

'Where are the wagons?' Moran asked.

'They are about three miles from here. Just follow my tracks through the brush and you will come up with them.'

Moran lifted a hand in acknowledgement and Gomez touched spurs to his mount and continued on his way. Moran motioned with his pistol and Hackett kicked his horse into motion. They went on, and covered more than two miles before they heard the sound of shooting ahead.

'That sounds like trouble,' said Hackett, reining in.

'Keep moving and we'll check it out,' Moran rapped, 'and don't forget my warning. If you try anything, I'll kill you.'

Hackett scowled and went on, pushing his horse into a canter. Moran stayed just behind, and they crashed through the brush. There had been a dozen shots fired in quick succession, but now an ominous silence reigned. Moran wondered why a simple chore such as recovering stolen supplies should have become so complicated . . .

Avery had no warning of trouble. Waiting for Hackett's return, he hunkered down beside the wagons in a small depression out of the direct rays of the sun. He heard nothing until a fusillade of shots broke the silence, and ducked when his hat was sent flying from his head. He drew his pistol and lay hunched in the brush, waiting for a break in the shooting before daring to raise his head.

When silence returned he eased up on his elbows to look around, and saw several mounted Mexicans riding towards him in a skirmish line, pistols and rifles levelled at the spot where he was hiding. An old campaigner, Avery guessed the Mexicans figured they had killed him, and he kept low, waiting for the right moment to catch them wrong-footed.

One of the Mexicans was making for the wagons. Avery lifted his pistol. He had not expected Mexican bandits to strike north of the border, and assumed that these were no ordinary bandits and that they had prior knowledge of the supplies. He wished Hackett would return. Hackett had said something about trouble for Gonzalez brewing in Mexico because of a disagreement within his gang, and he wondered if this was a breakaway group after the guns.

Avery triggered his Colt. The Mexican intent on reaching the wagons uttered a cry and fell off his horse. Avery changed position quickly, diving to his left as shooting exploded, and the brush was raked with flying lead. He arose and fired three shots at the riders before dropping back into cover to reload his pistol. He moved again, and was ready to continue his resistance when he caught the sound of hoofs approaching from behind. A sigh of relief escaped him — Hackett was coming back.

The next instant Hackett appeared. Avery risked a glance in his direction, caught a glimpse of someone behind him and assumed that it was Corporal Allen. He pushed himself up slightly to observe the Mexicans and a bullet smacked into his chest well below the right shoulder. Pain lashed him, his pistol spun out of his hand, and he twisted and fell on his face in the brush.

Hackett reined in and dived out of his saddle, hitting the ground hard beside Avery. He snatched up Avery's pistol and started shooting at the Mexicans. Moran reined in. He could see only four riders and triggered his deadly pistol, the shots hammering swiftly. The Mexicans were taken by surprise; two of them fell out their saddles.

Moran reined in. Gun smoke was thick in his nostrils. He swung his pistol but the surviving Mexicans turned their horses and disappeared into dense brush. Gun echoes faded slowly to a faint grumble on the far horizon. Hackett stood up with Avery's pistol in his hand, and grinned as he aimed the gun at Moran, who was turning to cover him. Hackett squeezed the trigger, but his face changed expression quickly when the hammer struck an empty chamber. He squeezed the trigger several more times without result, and then, with an expression of disgust on his face, he tossed the gun to the ground and raised his hands.

'How long have you been in the army?' Moran demanded. 'Didn't they teach you to count your shots?'

'It was heat of the moment stuff,' Hackett countered sullenly.

'So do something useful,' Moran replied. 'Check Avery. Is he hit hard?'

Hackett dropped to one knee beside the unconscious Avery and looked him over. He arose, shaking his head.

'He won't see the day out,' he said. 'The slug looks like it hit him in the lung.'

'Do what you can for him,' Moran ordered. 'We'll take him with us until he dies. Put him across his saddle, and hurry it up. We must turn the wagons around and get out of here fast. Those Mexicans will be back with reinforcements.'

'You expect me to help you take the

supplies back?' Hackett shook his head.

'You've got a choice,' Moran smiled tensely. 'You can help me or stay here afoot. I guess you know what will happen if you do stay.'

Hackett showed his teeth in a snarl and turned back to Avery. Moran moved in close but did not dismount. He held his gun in his right hand, the muzzle covering Hackett. When Hackett opened Avery's shirt and exposed the wound, Moran looked at it, gauging the degree of seriousness. He decided Avery was dying — would probably not recover consciousness.

'Put him on his horse,' Moran said. 'Then get up on the lead wagon and return to the north. I'll drive the second wagon, and if you try to get away I'll shoot you dead.'

'You're loco if you think we can get away now the Mexes have pinpointed us,' Hackett protested.

'We have no alternative but to try, so get moving. Tie your horse to the rear of the front wagon. I'll cover our rear.

And don't get any ideas about escaping. I've hunted you down once and I can do it again. You put yourself into this position, Hackett, and I'm the one who is gonna get you out, so set to and don't try any tricks.'

Hackett shook his head. 'We'll both be dead before morning,' he said. 'The Mexes will be back. There's a power struggle going on in Gonzalez's set-up, and those who have turned against him are after these supplies and guns. The only way we can survive is to leave everything here for them to pick up while we get clear. We can save ourselves, but no way can we get the supplies back. So let's make a run for it. I don't want to die in this godforsaken hole.'

'You've got no call to think of your future,' Moran replied. 'You're dead, whatever comes up. If the Mexicans don't get you then I'll take you back to Fort Broderick, where you'll stand trial for murdering Major Bixby, and I guess you know how that will end.'

'I'll do a deal with you.' Hackett's

voice became tinged with desperation. 'I'll help you get the wagons back to where they'll be safe and then you turn me loose.'

'No deals!' Moran shook his head. 'Get to it before the Mexicans show up again. We don't need to fight it out with them. And remember what I said about trying to escape. You brought the supplies out, and you're gonna help me take them back where they belong.'

Hackett put Avery across his saddle and then mounted his horse, holding the reins of Avery's mount in his left hand. He rode to where the wagons were standing, hitched the two saddle horses to the rear of the first wagon, and then climbed into the driving seat of the lead wagon. He whipped the team, turned the wagon around in a lumbering circle, and headed back north, shouting encouragement to the horses.

Moran tied his horse behind the second wagon, sprang into the driving seat, and followed Hackett closely. While they travelled back the way the supplies had come, Moran stayed alert. He kept a watch on their rear, and became hopeful of their chances of escape as they continued without incident. When Hackett halted later, Moran reined in, drew his gun and went forward to find Hackett sitting motionless on his seat.

'You're in trouble,' Hackett said. 'I've just thought of something. We ain't got enough fodder to sustain the horses. The Mexicans were supposed to provide feed on the other side of the Big Muddy, and they ain't gonna help us now so we ain't got one chance in a hundred. There's no grazing around here for miles. So what are you gonna do?'

Moran glanced around. There were no signs of pursuit by the Mexicans, and that was all he was concerned with at that moment. He considered the problem and came to an immediate decision.

'We'll hide the guns and ammunition,' he decided, 'and I can bring a detail back to collect them later.'

'Where do you reckon to hide them around here?' Hackett demanded. 'You'd have more luck trying to hide a hen from a hungry coyote! The Mexes will be back, and they won't miss a thing. Our tracks are plain to see.'

'There's a gully where I made camp last night,' Moran mused. 'I think it will do for our purpose. Get moving, and keep going now. We need to get everything out of sight.'

'The Mexes are desperate to get their hands on the guns.' Hackett shook his head, 'You're making a big mistake. We'll lose everything, including our lives.'

'Your life was forfeit from the moment Major Bixby was killed,' Moran observed.

Hackett got down from his seat. 'I'd better check Avery,' he said.

They went to the back of the wagon and Moran covered Hackett as he checked the sergeant.

'He's dead,' Hackett announced. 'We'll leave him here.' He grinned at Moran. 'Perhaps the Mexes will bury him.'

Moran rode close and checked the body sprawled across the saddle. Avery was indeed dead. He suppressed a sigh and went back to the second wagon, pausing to look for signs of pursuit. When he saw nothing suspicious he shook his head doubtfully. The Mexicans would surely come, and when they did they would have big odds on their side.

3

Rosita Gonzalez rode as if she had glimpsed the Devil on her back trail. She was gripped by desperation, and kept looking over her shoulder for signs of pursuit. The shooting she had heard warned her that trouble was close behind, and she wondered if she would be safe even if she reached her aunt's ranch. If she had been able to wait for her beloved Alfredo before fleeing from her father she would have avoided trouble, but she and Alfredo had been held as prisoners for weeks at her father's rancho before she managed to elude the guards and escape.

The horse suddenly changed its pace and began to limp. A groan escaped Rosita as she dismounted. She led the animal forward and noted that it was favouring its left foreleg. She bent to examine the swollen fetlock, and then straightened and looked around. She was relieved to see no signs of pursuit and felt a stab of relief in the back of her mind. But she had real trouble now: she was still some twenty miles from her aunt's home, and it looked as if she would have to walk the rest of the way. She set out resolutely, leading the limping horse, and tried not to think of the distance she had to cover. The brush was difficult to traverse on foot, and she did not think her moccasins would endure the punishment they would inevitably receive.

She covered three miles before she was compelled to rest. A big canteen was hanging from the saddle horn, and she drank sparingly. She looked around again. She had been running from the four bandits who had followed her from Chihuahua. At first she had thought they had been sent by her father to take her back to him, but when she had seen them on her back trail she had recognized them as men who had joined the group that had broken away from her father's bandit army because of his political ambitions, and she guessed they wanted to capture her in order to put pressure on her father.

Her meeting with the men running stolen army supplies into Mexico had given her a respite from her pursuers. After informing the *gringos* of the preparations her father had made for them when they crossed the border, she had asked for their help against her pursuers, but they had decided not to tackle the four Mexicans chasing her. She had fled on foot from their camp before daybreak, desperate to cover the last miles to the sanctuary of her aunt's ranch in the north. Then she had met the big *gringo* who had given her the horse and sent her on her way. But now she was afoot, and did not know if all four of her pursuers had been killed.

She continued resolutely, leading the horse, her thoughts turning on the situation as she knew it. She had broken away from her father because he would not let her marry Alfredo Gomez, but now she was faced with the task of freeing the man she loved from her father's clutches. She stumbled, almost fell, and, when she straightened, a movement to her right attracted her gaze and her heart seemed to miss a beat when she saw a man on a black horse emerging from the brush. She recognized Tomas Aguilar, one of the four men who had been pursuing her, and froze in shock as he came forward, his right hand resting on the butt of his holstered pistol.

'You have led me a pretty dance, Rosita,' he called, 'and you will pay for it before this is done.'

'Why were you chasing after me?' she demanded. 'I won't return to my father's rancho. If you take me back I shall flee again.'

'You'll be lucky to see Gonzalez again,' Aguilar responded with a taut smile, his dark eyes cold and hard, like black stones from the bottom of a creek. 'He will pay with his life for his change of attitude. His talk of revolution is flooding the countryside with

50

rurales, who are restricting the activities of honest bandits. But with Gonzalez dead, the *rurales* will go away and we can resume our way of life. So give me no trouble. I am with Sanchez now, and you will be returned to your home when Gonzalez has paid for his treachery. You will draw him into a trap, and when he is dead, you will be able to return to Alfredo.'

'Where is Alfredo?' she demanded. 'Is my father still holding him prisoner?'

'I do not know where he is.' Aguilar shrugged. 'He escaped from Gonzalez after you left. No doubt he will attempt to find you, but if he shows up on our trail with the intention of freeing you then I will kill him. So come along without trouble. The sooner we get this done the sooner you will be free.'

'I will take no part in causing the death of my father,' Rosita said fiercely, her dark eyes glinting.

Aguilar tapped the butt of his holstered pistol and smiled. 'The choice is yours. Come quietly with me or die where you stand.'

She sensed that he was deadly serious, and knew there was no profit in facing death in this wilderness. She nodded.

'I will ride with you, but my horse is lame.'

'We will get you another horse. You will have to ride that one until it drops. Do not attempt to escape, Rosita, because I will certainly kill you if I have to.'

She mounted her horse and set her heels against its flanks. The animal limped badly but they made progress. Aguilar followed her closely, his right hand resting lightly on the butt of his holstered gun. Rosita looked around, filled with desperation. The news that Alfredo Gomez had escaped from her father was good, for she knew that he would leave no stone unturned in his search for her. She had told Alfredo many times before escaping from her father that she would go to her aunt in Texas, and Alfredo had promised to seek her there.

Aguilar had no wish to confront Slade Moran again, and rode to the west to bypass the supply wagons at a safe distance on his way back to the border. The trip would be fraught with danger because Gonzalez had many sympathizers despite his political leanings.

Rosita's horse limped on for several miles before halting and refusing to continue. She dismounted. Aguilar checked the animal and shook his head.

'It is finished,' he said, drawing his pistol.

Rosita dismounted, removed the saddle from the animal, and stepped in front of it when Aguilar lifted his gun to shoot it.

'Leave it,' she said firmly.

He shrugged and returned his pistol to its holster. 'Come and get up behind me,' he commanded. 'We must make haste to cross the border.'

She moved towards him, and, as he reached a hand down to her, she heard the sudden rapid beat of hoofs close by. She turned, and saw three heavily armed *gringos* appearing out of the brush, each holding a levelled pistol. Hoofs sounded from behind, and she turned her head quickly to see three more riders appearing. Aguilar reached for his pistol, but realized that he had no chance against the newcomers and raised his hands.

The riders surrounded them and sat motionless with menacing guns. They were tough, hard-looking men, each wearing the badge of the Texas Rangers. One of them, apparently their leader, holstered his pistol and leaned his hands on his saddle horn. He was a big man, powerful, and his abrupt manner exuded toughness. His bronzed face was set in harsh lines, and his dark eyes were the coldest Rosita had ever seen.

'I'm Captain Seth Manning of the Texas Rangers,' he declared in a rasping tone. 'What are you two doing here?'

'I'm Rosita Gonzalez, Captain, and I was making for my aunt's rancho before Aguilar here stopped me and decided to take me back to Mexico and my father.'

'Acting against your will?' Manning's dark eyes narrowed as he regarded Aguilar. 'What is your business on this side of the border?'

'It is a personal matter,' Aguilar replied.

'Kidnapping is a serious matter either side of the line,' Manning observed. 'Get rid of your gun, mister.'

Aguilar drew his pistol, using forefinger and thumb only, and dropped the weapon to the ground.

'You've come from Mexico?' Manning continued, looking at Rosita. 'Did you see two supply wagons south of here?'

'Yes. I stayed at their camp last night,' she replied.

'How many men did you see?'

'There were three,' Rosita replied.

Manning twisted in his saddle. 'Bennett, take Ross and Wade with you and go get a fix on those wagons. Don't show yourselves. I'll come up with you shortly.'

Three of the riders turned away and

55

disappeared into the brush. Manning returned his attention to Rosita.

'You are running away from your father,' he said. 'Tell me why.'

'I left home because my father would not let me marry the man I love. I escaped, and my father sent four men to take me back. When I left the wagon camp this morning I was afoot, and Aguilar had three men with him. One of the wagon guards tried to kill an army captain who was tracking them, and was shot. The captain gave me a horse, and as I rode away there was more shooting. It seems that Aguilar and his men attacked the soldier and he shot it out with them. Aguilar caught up with me just before you appeared. He was going to take me back to Mexico, but not to my father. He said he was going to hold me hostage to get an advantage over my father.'

'Who is your father?' Manning demanded. 'It sounds like he's important.'

'He is Fernando Gonzalez, the bandit,' Aguilar cut in. 'He is planning a revolution across the border, and some of us plan to stop him. We need Rosita to put pressure on him.'

'I've heard of Fernando Gonzalez.' Manning frowned. 'Who is your aunt and where is her ranch, *señorita*?'

'She is Señora Perdita Ruiz, Captain.'

'I know her well.' Manning motioned to one of his attentive men. 'Chuck, escort the *señorita* to her aunt's home and check she will be welcome there. If she isn't then see that she gets to where ever she wants to go, and don't come back until she is settled safe somewhere.'

'Thank you, Captain.' Rosita glanced at Aguilar, whose face was expressionless. 'What will you do with him? He will come after me again if you set him free.'

'He'll tag along with us for a spell before I see him back across the border,' said Manning, 'and if he shows his face around here again I'll make him mighty sorry.'

The Ranger called Chuck slid his

foot out of his left-hand stirrup and motioned for Rosita to mount behind him. She obeyed with alacrity, and clung to his belt as he spurred his horse and sent it galloping through the brush.

Captain Manning rode south behind the three men he had sent to locate the stolen wagons, and the two remaining Rangers followed him closely, one of them riding herd on the hapless Aguilar. They moved swiftly through familiar territory, alert and ready for trouble.

Up ahead, Ranger Bennett had spotted the two wagons being driven into a wide gully. He saw Moran and Hackett, and halted to remain in cover. He frowned while he wondered why the wagons were no longer pushing south. The Rangers had been riding hell for leather to prevent the stolen supplies from reaching the border, and now, when the wagons were on the point of crossing the Rio Grande, it looked as if they had turned back.

'Ross,' Bennett said. 'Ride back to the captain and tell them about this.

We'll wait here and keep an eye on them.'

Ross nodded and dismounted to lead his horse away. Moments later he remounted and rode off. Bennett tethered his horse and moved forward, accompanied by Wade, and they crouched in the brush to watch Moran emerge from the gully and stand in its entrance to look around.

'I wonder what they're up to,' Bennett mused. 'From all the reports, they were pushing hard for the border, so why are they holing up in that gully?'

'Do you want me to go and ask them?' Wade asked with a grin.

Bennett gave an answering smile. 'We'll just obey orders,' he replied. 'Get into cover and watch.'

They faded into the brush and remained motionless.

* * *

Moran was sweating. He turned back into the gully, thankful that it was wide enough to accommodate the wagons. He had been expecting an attack, but felt safe for the moment, and there were no signs of activity anywhere. He turned and followed the wagons as Hackett drove the lead vehicle deeper into the gully. The deserter reined in suddenly and jumped down from his seat. He paused and gazed at Moran.

'Do you hope to hide all this stuff in here?' Hackett demanded.

'Just keep going up the gully,' Moran directed. 'There's a bend ahead with a steep bank on one side that has been underscored by water, and with any luck we should be able to drop the bank down over the entire load.'

'And then what?'

'We'll get out of here and I'll come back with an army detail to collect it later.'

'Do you reckon the Mexes ain't watching our every move?' Hackett laughed harshly. 'You ain't ever gonna get out of this gully. Gonzalez wants this shipment mighty bad, and what he wants he gets.

He's had men watching our every move ever since we left the fort. You ain't got a hope.'

'I'd rather be in my boots than yours,' Moran confided. 'Whatever chances I've got, you have even less. Now get on, and with a bit of luck we might both get out of here alive.'

Hackett shrugged and climbed back on the wagon. He urged the team forward and Moran dropped back to the second wagon. He followed Hackett, who halted again when he reached the bend in the gully, where the deep depression carved by rushing water centuries before had been forced to the left. Moran studied the area. The water had undercut the bank at the elbow, and he fancied there was just enough room to place the weapons and ammunition under cover. With the bank dropped, the vital weapons would be out of sight under tons of rock.

'How are you gonna cover this stuff when we've unloaded it?' Hackett demanded.

'I have a list of everything you stole from the fort, and I know you took gunpowder, which I'll use to bring the bank down. So let's get to work and unload this stuff. The sooner we bury it the sooner we can get out of here.'

They worked together unloading the wagons and placing the supplies in the undercut. Moran sweated. His nerves were on edge. He had to watch Hackett all the time in case the deserter should try to escape, and also keep an eye on his surroundings. He was expecting another attack from the Mexicans, but the heavy silence remained unbroken, and eventually all the supplies were unloaded and stored beneath the overhang. Hackett sat down on a rock and wiped sweat from his forehead. Heat had packed inside the gully and there was no breeze to dissipate it.

Moran stepped back and looked at the side of the gully overhanging the supplies. His keen eyes spotted a natural fault about twenty feet above the undercut, where two huge rocks were leaning against each other with a small cavity beneath them. His experienced eye picked out the cavity as being suitable for his plan. He picked up a small keg of gunpowder, located detonators and fuse wire, and made Hackett take them up a faint game trail to the cavity while he covered the man with his pistol. When Hackett returned, Moran bound him, left him lying hog-tied and helpless on the floor of the gully, and ascended to the cavity.

With the keg of gunpowder in position, Moran used his knife to put a hole in the lid. He attached fuse wire to a detonator, which he inserted into the keg. He was jamming the extra space in the cavity with small rocks when a voice called to him from below, and he looked down to see two strangers staring up at him and covering him with pistols. His eyes narrowed when he saw that each was wearing a Texas Ranger badge — a small silver star in a silver circle.

'Get rid of your weapons and then come on down,' Captain Manning called. 'Don't attempt to light that fuse. You've got some big explaining to do, and then some.'

Moran tossed down his gun and knife. He left the fuse wire dangling and descended into the gully. Hackett was grinning. Captain Manning checked Moran for hidden weapons, removed the gun from the back of his belt, which he had taken from Hackett, and took the .41 derringer from his jacket pocket before stepping back.

'So what gives?' Manning demanded.

'I'm Captain Moran of the Special Investigation Department of the Army of Interior. These supplies were stolen from Fort Broderick some weeks ago by three army deserters. My prisoner is Corporal Hackett, the only surviving deserter. The wagons have been attacked by Mexicans, and I decided to hide the supplies here until I can return with an army detail to move them to safety.'

'You have papers to prove your identity?' Manning asked.

Moran produced his ID and Manning

nodded when he saw it.

'I received a telegram from Ranger headquarters before I headed in this direction,' Manning said, 'alerting me to the theft from Fort Broderick, and naming you as the investigating officer. I'm pleased to make your acquaintance, Captain, and I have fresh orders for you. I picked up a telegram in Del Rio, addressed to you. My own orders are to apprehend the deserters and prevent the supplies from falling into the hands of Fernando Gonzalez, the bandit who is organizing a revolution south of the border. We have been riding hell for leather to catch up with these wagons before they could cross the river.'

Moran frowned as he took the telegram that Manning held out to him. It was signed by his immediate superior, Colonel Wakefield, and ordered him to contact and hand over the stolen supplies to a Mexican named Pedro Sanchez, who controlled the group in opposition to Fernando Gonzalez.

'Good news, I hope,' said Manning.

'A change of orders,' Moran replied, 'which means a change of plan. I have to hand these supplies over to a group of Mexicans led by one Pedro Sanchez.' He picked up his pistol and knife.

'Are you kidding?' Manning regarded Moran with suspicion in his eyes. 'There's a revolution building up south of the border, and if these supplies fall into the wrong hands there will be hell to pay.'

'My orders are to hand the supplies over to the men opposing the revolution.' Moran handed the telegram to the Ranger captain.

'I know Fernandez Gonzalez is bossing the revolutionaries.' Manning scratched the stubble on his chin. 'And I've heard of Pedro Sanchez. How will you contact him?'

'He shouldn't be too difficult to find.' Moran shrugged his shoulders. 'What I have to do is ensure that these supplies are safe until I can hand them over.'

'Well, I can't help you.' Manning shook his head. 'I'll have to head back now we've tracked you down. Maybe you'd better drop that bank down on those supplies. Sanchez can dig them out when he needs them. I can take your prisoner along and drop him off at the jail in Del Rio. That will get him out of your hair. You helped Rosita Gonzalez to escape some Mexicans this morning. She is the daughter of the man leading the revolution. And I picked up a man named Aguilar who had taken the girl prisoner. He said he is working with the men opposing Gonzalez, so perhaps you'd better talk to him. He might save you some time and trouble.'

'Rosita mentioned her father.' Moran nodded. 'I was attacked by four Mexicans this morning, and killed three of them. The fourth one I turned loose. He might be one of Sanchez's men. Where is he?'

Manning jerked a thumb along the gully and they moved in that direction, A ranger took charge of Hackett. Moran recognized Aguilar when he saw the Mexican, and Aguilar shrugged at the sight of Moran.

'I told you to head on out when I turned you loose earlier,' Moran said heavily. 'You disobeyed me and took out after Rosita, huh? Were you planning on taking her back to Gonzalez?'

'No,' Aguilar replied. 'I am with the men who do not want a revolution.'

'Do you know Pedro Sanchez?' Moran asked.

'But of course,' Aguilar grinned. 'He is our leader against Gonzalez. It was his idea to take Rosita and use her as a lever against her father.'

'Will you take a message to Sanchez?' Moran asked.

Aguilar frowned. 'What have you to say that would interest him? It would be better if you let Rosita ride with me. With her in our hands we could stop the revolution. You have prevented the supplies reaching Gonzalez, which he is relying on.'

'My orders are to give the supplies to Sanchez,' Moran said.

Aguila's eyes widened, and then he laughed. 'That is good. Gonzalez paid a lot of dollars for those supplies, and you will give them to us for nothing?'

'I'm obeying orders,' Moran said, 'and I'll want to meet Sanchez before I hand anything over to him.'

'Give me my gun and I'll go back across the river. It will take me some days to get to Sanchez. If you camp this side of the river I'll come back to you. But you must guard against Gonzalez. His men are watching you, and they will not let you hand the supplies to Sanchez.'

'Don't worry about the supplies,' Moran said. 'Bring Sanchez back with you and he can take what he wants.'

'It would be good if you let me take Rosita Gonzalez with me,' Aguilar said hopefully.

'No dice,' Manning cut in. 'Rosita is heading for her aunt's ranch and I'll be dropping in on her when I ride back that way. You'd better get moving, Aguilar. You've got enough to do as it is without saddling yourself with the girl.'

The Mexican turned away. Moran watched him ride off, wondering just what his new orders had let him in for. But he could not query them; his duty was to obey implicitly.

'I'll get moving,' Manning said. He whirled around when a shot sounded from the direction Aguilar had taken. 'What in hell was that?'

Moran turned also, and reached for his holstered gun. He saw Aguilar in the distance, reeling in his saddle. Gun smoke was drifting from the nearby brush. The Rangers started shooting into the brush. Two jumped on their horses and galloped toward Aguilar, who pitched out of his saddle and fell heavily to the ground. Moran ran into the gully and fetched his horse from the back of the second wagon. He sprang into leather and rode quickly to where Aguilar was down. The shooting had died away now, and sullen echoes were growling in the distance.

4

Aguilar was lying on his back. His eyes were closed but he was conscious, his eyelids flickering. Moran dismounted and bent over the Mexican. Blood was oozing from a bullet hole high up in the right side of his chest. Shooting began again, and Moran ducked as a bullet crackled over his head. He turned his attention to the fight that erupted. The Rangers were firing rapidly into the brush. Gun smoke drifted quickly on the breeze. Moran saw several riders in the background, all shooting towards the gully: they were Mexicans. He lifted his pistol and returned fire, not knowing if they were men who rode with Sanchez or Gonzalez. Whoever they were, they wanted to fight.

Captain Manning shouted orders to his Rangers, and the hard-faced law men headed into the brush, shooting as they went, riding straight at the Mexicans. Gunfire blasted and echoes fled to the horizon. Moran triggered his Colt, aiming for fleeting figures, and saw two of the Mexicans drop out of their saddles. A bullet from his right crackled in his ear in a near miss, and he swung his pistol. The Rangers disappeared into the brush, and the volume of shooting rose to a higher level as they clashed with the men from across the border.

Moran reloaded his pistol and returned to Aguilar. The Rangers seemed to have the measure of the Mexicans. He dropped to one knee beside the wounded man. Aguilar's eyes were open now, and he tried to sit up but Moran pushed him back.

'Lie still while I check you out,' Moran commanded.

Aguilar relaxed. 'I saw those who started the shooting,' he said. 'They are from Gonzalez. They want those supplies. There will be a hundred of Gonzalez's men around here before the sun goes down.'

'They won't get anything.' Moran opened Aguilar's shirt and examined the bullet wound. 'It looks like you'll be OK,' he mused. 'You've got a broken rib, it looks like, but the bullet appears to have missed your lung. It clipped the rib and was deflected outwards, which is lucky for you. Stop talking and lie still. I'll come back to you shortly with some bandaging to fix you up.'

He swung into his saddle and took out after the Rangers. Occasional shots were still being fired in the distance. The fight had spread through the brush. Moran guessed the Mexicans had not expected the Rangers to be around and had fled in the face of superior fire. But he knew they would return with a force sufficient to deal with any opposition. He reined about and went back to Aguilar, aware that there was nothing he could do about Gonzalez.

'I must get to Sanchez,' Aguilar said. 'Put me in a saddle and point me towards the river. I'll fetch Sanchez and some of his men here for the supplies.'

'Gonzalez's men are out in force,' Moran warned. 'Run into them, they'll kill you.'

'I'll head upriver a couple of miles and then cross.' Aguilar pushed himself into a sitting position. His forehead was beaded with sweat, his swarthy face pale beneath its tan. 'Help me to my feet and I'll get moving.'

'You need treatment, or you won't get far,' Moran replied. 'Take it easy. I've got some medical stuff in my saddle-bags.'

Aguilar struggled to his feet. 'I can ride,' he insisted. 'It is important that I get some men in here.' He pulled away from Moran's outstretched hand, staggered to where his horse was standing with trailing reins, and hauled himself into the saddle.

Moran shook his head as the Mexican rode off, swaying in his saddle. Moran's duty was to see that the supplies reached Sanchez, and he dared not leave the mouth of the gully in case some of Gonzalez's men sneaked around the Rangers and tried to snatch them. He led his horse into the gully and tethered it. Hackett was lying just inside where the Rangers had left him hog-tied, and Moran went to his side.

'You sure started something when you stole those supplies,' Moran observed. 'You were in touch with Gonzalez before you deserted, huh? How come you trusted a bandit?'

'He wanted supplies and we got them for him,' Hackett replied. 'It only got complicated when Gonzalez decided to start a revolution. We had a down pay-ment from him on the weapons, and now he wants the guns.'

'He's gonna be disappointed, if I have anything to do with it.' Moran spoke firmly. He drew his pistol and checked its load while considering what he should do. If Gonzalez's men looked likely to snatch the supplies then he would have to detonate the charge he had placed and bury the vital guns under tons of rock. That action would buy him some much needed time. His mind cleared when he realized that he had no options; his duty was plain.

Four riders appeared to the left and began shooting at him. Moran was expecting the Rangers to return, but these were Mexicans. He dived into cover, his pistol lifting into the aim. He glanced around, and his eyes narrowed to slits when he spotted a rider coming towards the gully from the north. He just had time to recognize the girl, Rosita, before being caught up in a furious spate of shooting. The Mexicans came at him recklessly, bent low in their saddles and shooting rapidly.

Moran returned fire. Sweat trickled down his face. He swung his pistol, allowed for the movement of the nearest rider, and squeezed his trigger. The pistol recoiled and the Mexican fell sideways out of his saddle, blood spurting from his throat. Moran ducked as questing lead crackled around him. He changed position and came up into the aim again, firing rapidly. The Mexicans swung away in the face of his accurate shooting, and Moran hit another of them as they fled into nearby cover. He watched with impassive gaze as the lifeless body thumped on the hard ground.

The shooting faded away to nothing. Echoes sounded sullen in the distance. Moran could hear remote shots as the Rangers continued hunting down targets. Hoofs pounded to his right and he turned his head quickly to see Rosita coming up fast. She was riding the Ranger's horse, and dismounted as the animal slithered to a dust-raising halt. She came running to the mouth of the gully with slugs snarling around her as she was spotted by the skulking Mexicans.

Moran reached out a long arm and grasped the girl, pulling her into cover. His gaze was on the brush ahead, his pistol ready for action.

'What happened to you?' he asked without looking at her. 'Where's that

Ranger you rode off with?'

'He was shot,' Rosita replied. 'Three Mexicans ambushed us. I recognized one of them. They were my father's men. The Ranger was not killed instantly; he shot it out with them while I rode back this way. I did not know what else to do.'

'You should have kept heading north,' Moran said. 'It would have been safer.'

'But I would have been caught,' she protested. 'Who are these men shooting at you?'

'Some more of your father's gang, I guess.' Moran fired at a fleeting figure that showed momentarily in the brush. Gun smoke blew into his face and he exhaled heavily to clear his lungs. His eyes watered and he blinked rapidly. It looked as if the Mexicans were getting ready to make another attack. He thumbed fresh shells into his pistol.

'Aguilar was one of my father's most trusted men, but now he is riding with Sanchez,' she mused. 'Is Sanchez after the guns?'

'He's gonna get them, if I have anything to do with it,' Moran said. 'Keep your head down.'

'Don't trust Sanchez,' Rosita gasped as she dropped flat. 'He was born a bandit and will die a bandit.'

Two Mexicans appeared from the brush and came toward the gully, shooting rapidly without aiming. Moran kept low and lifted his gun. He drew a bead on the nearest and fired. His slug slammed the Mexican out of his saddle, and the second man whirled away again, heading back into cover. Moran hastened him on his way with two shots.

The distant shooting had faded away completely. Moran watched the brush, and presently, seeing riders coming forward, readied himself for further action. Then he recognized Manning, the Ranger captain, and lowered his pistol. The Rangers came up fast and dismounted in front of the gully. Moran got to his feet.

'We drove them off,' Manning said.

'They went across the river. But they'll be back, I don't doubt. They sure want those supplies!' He saw Rosita in the background and his expression changed. 'What are you doing here?' he demanded.

Rosita explained and Manning uttered an oath under his breath.

'Well, that does it,' he said. 'We'll have to head back and look for Chuck. They were men from your father doing the shooting, huh?'

'Yes. I recognized some of them,' Rosita replied.

Manning turned to Moran. 'I'm sorry I've got to pull out,' he apologized. 'But I'll leave Bennett with you, just in case any more greasers show up. I'll take your prisoner along with me and lodge him in a cell in Del Rio.'

'Thanks,' Moran replied. 'And send a wire to my headquarters when you get the chance. Tell them I'm following their orders. Confirm that the guns will go to Sanchez, and ask for an army patrol to be sent here.' He turned to Rosita. The girl's brown face was strained, her eyes filled with shock. 'I've got some good news for you.' He told her about meeting Alfredo Gomez, and saw her eyes flare with sudden hope.

'That is the best news in the world,' she said. 'He will go to my aunt's ranch for me.'

Captain Manning prepared to ride out. He told Bennett to remain with Moran, ordered another of his men to pick up a spare mount for Hackett, and then set off, taking Hackett and Rosita with him. Moran checked his pistol as he watched them fade into the brush to the north. When they had disappeared he holstered his gun and looked around to check his position, aware that the Mexicans would be back. The atmosphere was vibrant with hostility. Bennett checked his pistol and then holstered it. He peered out from the gully mouth and watched the brush.

'I figure to stay with you until sundown,' Bennett remarked. 'After that I'll have to get moving.'

'I've got an explosive charge set to bury the supplies,' Moran mused. 'I think I'd better use it now, while there are no Mexicans around.'

'So you're gonna give the guns to Sanchez?' Bennett demanded.

'I follow orders.' Moran grimaced. 'But that doesn't necessarily mean that I agree with what I have to do.'

'Gonzalez is known along the border as a bandit. Now he's aiming to become the next president of Mexico,' Bennett mused. 'And because Sanchez is setting himself up against Gonzalez you're ordered to hand over the weapons to him. So what happens if Sanchez beats Gonzalez, and then decides to try for the presidency?'

'That's the way it goes.' Moran shook his head. 'Thankfully, I don't make policy. If the situation you mention arises then I'll probably be ordered to take the guns back from Sanchez.' He peered out of the gully. There was no movement in the surrounding brush. 'Give me a hand to back the two wagons down here. Then you can stay put with them while I bury the supplies. Afterwards I'll pull out with you and head for Del Rio. I can wire headquarters from there and bring in soldiers to guard the supplies until they can be handed over to Sanchez.'

'I wouldn't waste too much time,' Bennett replied, looking around. 'Those Mexes will be back soon, thicker than fleas on a hound dog.'

Moran led the way and walked up the gully to the spot where the supplies had been unloaded in the undercut. They backed the wagons down to the entrance. Bennett remained with the teams. Moran went back to the undercut and checked his preparations for detonating the charge. Satisfied that he had not overlooked anything, he lit the fuse and then dropped down into the gully. He ensured that the fuse was burning steadily before heading back down to the gully entrance to join Bennett.

They crouched in cover, waiting tensely for the explosion, and it came like a thunderclap of doom. Smoke billowed and a storm of rocks and dust sailed skywards. Tremendous echoes were hurled into the vast distance, and seemed to go on forever. Then rocks came crashing down in a vicious shower, and Moran winced with pain when the wound in his leg was struck. He ducked and closed his eyes until the storm passed.

When silence returned, Moran got up and went back up the gully to check the effects of the explosion, choking in the dust cloud that swirled around. The charge had brought down the whole side of the gully and tons of broken rock covered the supplies completely. The gully itself was blocked. Moran gazed around critically, and hoped that no one could guess the supplies were buried here. He walked down to the entrance and found Bennett waiting for him with the horses.

'It's time to ride,' said the Ranger. 'I caught a glimpse of some Mexicans coming from the direction of the river.

We'd better get out of here.'

Moran shook his head. He was thinking hard about the situation and knew what he had to do.

'I can't leave,' he said firmly. 'I'll have to stick around here and keep the Mexicans away from those supplies. That's my job. If Captain Manning sends off a wire to army headquarters when he reaches Del Rio it will save me a long ride.'

'OK.' Bennett swung into his saddle. 'See you around.'

'Do me one last favour,' Moran said. 'Take these teams and wagons away from here. You can turn the horses loose a couple of miles on. Take them out of the wagons so they can fend for themselves.'

Bennett tied the team of the second wagon to the rear of the front one, mounted his horse, and, holding the lead rope of the leading team, set spurs to his mount and departed. Moran watched until Bennett disappeared to the north. He glanced around. The surrounding silence seemed filled with menace. He checked his pistol and rifle before leading his horse away to cover. Then he entered the gully, ascended to the spot where the supplies were buried, and climbed the pile of rocks that was blocking the gully. He settled down in cover at the top and waited for the Mexicans to return . . .

★ ★ ★

Aguilar clung to his saddle as he headed for the river. The pain in his chest was considerable, and he fought the urge to vacate his saddle and stretch out on the hard ground to find some relief, but he pressed a hand to the wound, gritted his teeth, and continued. There was a single thought in his head: he had to stay clear of Gonzalez's men, for they would shoot him out of hand. When he reached the river-bank he sprawled out of his saddle and crawled to the water's edge to slake his raging thirst. He saw riders in the distance, south of his position, using the main crossing from Mexico, and recognized them as Gonzalez's men. He decided to remain in cover until they were out of sight. He had to find some of his own men to convey to Sanchez a message about the arms and supplies.

He crawled back into the bushes where he had left his horse and relaxed with a sigh, his gaze on the figures moving across the river. When he saw a big man on a white stallion trailing along behind, he stiffened and drew his pistol, although he was way out of range. The man was Fernando Gonzalez, and Aguilar's fingers itched to fire a killing shot. But Gonzalez crossed the river and vanished from sight. Aguilar made an effort, dragged himself to his feet, swung into his saddle, and sent his horse into the river. He needed to contact Sanchez urgently, for it was obvious that Gonzalez was after the weapons.

★ ★ ★

Moran waited stolidly. Time was not important now. He welcomed the silence and the stillness. When he glimpsed movement near the entrance to the gully he crouched and watched intently. Two Mexicans appeared on foot, sneaking forward with rifles in their hands. Moran did not know if they were for Gonzalez or Sanchez. He held his fire, watching them. They came close to where the supplies were buried. Dust from the explosion was still drifting in the air. He studied the pile of rocks covering the supplies and saw that it was obvious an explosion had brought down the wall of the gully, and it would need little in the way of intelligence for someone to surmise that something was buried under the fallen rock.

The Mexicans stood and observed the scene for some minutes. Then one of them turned and went back the way they had come. Moran, perched twenty feet above the remaining man, drew his Colt and cocked it. The remaining

Mexican heard the ominous sound and looked up quickly. He dropped his rifle when he found himself covered by the muzzle of Moran's gun.

'Whose side are you on?' Moran demanded.

The Mexican's dark eyes narrowed as he considered the question. He glanced down the gully as if hopeful that some of his friends would appear and come to his aid.

'I ride for Gonzalez,' he replied at length. 'We are here for the guns. An arrangement was made with the men who own the guns. Some money was paid over. We have the rest of the money, and we want the guns. Are they buried here?'

'The men who stole the guns from the army have been killed or arrested, and they are out of it now,' Moran replied. 'The guns are going back to where they belong.'

'I think not.' The Mexican shrugged. 'Gonzalez is coming. He wants those guns, and will kill anyone who gets in his way. If you value your life you will ride away from here while you still can.'

Moran considered the situation, aware that he could not change his plan. He had to stay and prevent Gonzalez getting the supplies, even if it cost him his life. He had been given a definite order, and would obey it.

'You'd better get out of here,' he called to the Mexican. 'If I see you again I'll put a slug through you.'

The Mexican turned and hurried back down the gully. Silence came. Moran checked his weapons, it looked as if he was in for a hard fight. He glanced around, considering his position. The Mexicans would have to come at him from the entrance to the gully. They could not get above him from the sides because he was holding the high ground. He waited stolidly. An ominous silence seemed to close in around him as he watched the lower part of the gully. The Mexicans would have a hundred yards of bare ground to negotiate if they made a frontal attack.

Moran was satisfied. He was as ready as he could be. Time passed slowly, and his nerves tightened as he waited. He wiped sweat from his forehead and remained motionless.

The silence was suddenly shattered by several rifles firing from the entrance to the gully. Moran hunched his shoulders and tightened his grip on his rifle. Flying lead spattered the rocks about him as he looked eagerly for targets. The Mexicans were taking no chances. Gun smoke drifted on the bright air, and although Moran caught glimpses of furtive figures down below he did not get an opportunity to fire.

Time passed. The shadows in the gully moved slightly as the sun shifted in the brassy sky. The shooting had long since ceased, and Moran eased up a fraction behind his cover and kept a close watch on the entrance to the gully. He heard voices calling orders and instructions, but there was no move by the Mexicans to make a concerted attack on him.

Suddenly a rider appeared from the cover of rocks littering the entrance down below. He was a big Mexican astride a powerful white stallion. Moran covered him and waited. The rider pulled a pistol from his belt and tossed it on the ground, then did the same with his rifle. He sat for a moment gazing up at Moran's position, his swarthy face harshly set. He was big for a Mexican and was dressed in drab clothing. His face was dark and intent, his eyes filled with passion. He touched spurs to the flanks of his horse and came up the gully at a walk, his gaze never leaving the spot where Moran was waiting. Moran let his gaze flick around, looking for trouble from unexpected directions. But nothing was moving down there at the entrance.

When Gonzalez reached the spot where the supplies were buried he reined in and studied the area, shaking his head. Then he looked up to where Moran was waiting.

'Hey, *gringo*,' he called in a hoarse

tone, his thin lips twisting, spitting the words as if they burned his mouth. 'I am Fernando Gonzalez. Why have you done this to my property? I paid good US dollars to your soldiers for those supplies, and I need them now. Why do you push your nose into something that does not concern you?'

Moran did not reply. He kept Gonzalez covered and checked out the lower rims of the gully for any sign of Mexicans creeping forward to engage him. He saw nothing suspicious and returned his attention to Gonzalez.

'Talk to me, *gringo*. I hold your life in my hands. I have fifty men at the entrance down there, and if I drop my hat they will ride up here and stomp you into the dust. You cannot fight such odds, so why don't you get out of here and ride away?'

'I can't do that, Gonzalez,' Moran replied, his voice echoing slightly. 'I have an interest in those guns you're after, and I'm going to stop you collecting them. Why don't you ride back across the border where you belong? A big army detachment will be showing up here shortly, and if you're still around when they arrive they'll send you back to Mexico with your tail between your legs. You won't have the guns, but you and your men will be carrying plenty of lead between you. So take my advice — head on out and don't come back. It will be healthier for you to stay on your side of the river.'

Gonzalez shook his head. 'I am a simple man, *gringo*. I paid good money for the guns and I have come to collect them. Nothing will stop me — not even your army. It would be better for you to ride out and leave me to take what is mine. Think it over. If you do not leave then my men will ride up here and kill you. If you wish to die then that is all right by me. That is all I have to say.'

Gonzalez rode back down the gully. Moran watched him, prepared to fight to the death. He glanced at the upper slope of the gully to his rear, and common sense warned that he should withdraw before the Mexicans could cut him off. He needed to get clear of the gully, and was aware that Gonzalez had spoken the truth. If he did not pull out then he would be overrun. He sensed that now was the time to get moving. He reached a sudden decision and slid back from his position to climb down the reverse side of the tumbled rocks into the upper reaches of the gully. As he started running for the top end of the gully the Mexicans opened up a barrage of rifle fire at his former position.

Moran cleared the area while the gully below was deluged with indiscrimate fire. He estimated that Gonzalez had not lied about the number of men at his disposal, and was aware that if Captain Manning and his Texas Rangers had remained to back him they would have been shot out of existence.

By the time he reached the upper part of the gully the shooting had dwindled away to sporadic shots. Moran paused for breath and looked back to where he had dynamited the gully wall. He saw several Mexicans standing on top of the heap of jumbled rocks covering the supplies, and others already advancing up the gully to attack him.

Moran left the gully and crossed the high ground to his left. He began an arduous descent to the lower level and ran to where he had hidden his horse. When he saw the animal he halted in cover, for a Mexican was standing beside the bay, holding a pistol in his right hand. He began to stalk the man, but he saw two more Mexicans in cover nearby and paused to take stock.

Aware that he had no time to lose, Moran drew his pistol and fired at the Mexican standing beside the horse. The animal started nervously as the Mexican fell against it, and Moran started forward instantly, turning his pistol on the two Mexicans in cover. When slugs began snarling around them they jumped to their feet and began to shoot at him. Moran ignored their fire and continued to engage them.

A bullet tugged at the holster on Moran's right hip. He threw himself to the rough ground, his gun lined up on his target. He squeezed off a shot, saw one of the Mexicans fall, and turned his .45 on the second man. The crash of the shooting hammered into the distance. Moran was dimly aware that rifles had begun firing at him from the high ground he had recently vacated, and pushed himself to his feet and ran to his horse, trading shots with the surviving Mexican.

He had knee-hobbled his horse, and bent to jerk the short rope free of the animal's legs. A bullet snarled in his left ear as he straightened and he paused to draw a bead on the remaining Mexican, who was coming forward from cover. They fired simultaneously. Moran felt the slash of a slug creasing his left forearm and almost dropped his rifle but retained his hold. He saw the Mexican jerk and fall backwards.

But the Mexican was not finished.

He pushed himself up and cut loose with his pistol. His dusky face was shadowed by the wide brim of his sombrero. His thin lips were peeled back from his gleaming teeth in a snarl of defiance. He squeezed his trigger relentlessly and the weapon recoiled in his hand and spurted fire, smoke and death. Moran dropped into cover and waited for the man's hammer to strike an empty cartridge. His position was blasted by the accurate shooting.

When the shooting cut off suddenly, Moran leapt up to see the Mexican feverishly feeding fresh cartridges into his pistol. Moran levelled his .45, took careful aim, and squeezed his trigger just once. The Mexican dropped his gun and fell forward on to his face.

Moran sprang into his saddle and caught up the trailing reins. He thrust his rifle into the saddleboot and holstered his pistol. Rifle slugs were striking the ground around him in profusion. He glanced at the nearby skyline and saw a dozen Mexicans gathered there, all intent on shooting him. He spurred his horse and bent low over the animal's neck as it hit a gallop. Moments later he was in the clear and hidden by thick brush. The shooting petered out and an uneasy silence settled.

5

Captain Manning set a fast pace as he headed north, with Rosita guiding him back to where Chuck Lloyd had been ambushed. Reaching the area, the Rangers spread out to search the brush, and within minutes the fallen Ranger had been located. He was dead; shot several times. The Rangers buried him without ceremony, and Manning's weatherbeaten face was grim as they continued north on the trail to the little town of Del Rio.

By late evening they reached the fork that led to the ranch owned by Rosita's aunt, and Manning called a halt to give the horses a breather. Rosita spoke to the Ranger captain. 'I can get to my aunt's ranch quite easily alone from here, Captain,' she said.

Manning looked around. He nodded. 'You can go on from here, but not alone.' He glanced at his men. 'Wade, you ride with her and see her safe to the ranch, then come on to Del Rio.'

'Sure thing, Captain.' Wade tightened his cinch and stepped up into the saddle. Rosita spurred her horse and they rode off into the gathering shadows.

Manning went on then, riding faster, wanting to get to town. He was concerned about Moran fighting Mexicans on American soil.

The lights of the town beckoned them long before they reached the outskirts of Del Rio. When they hit the main street, Manning reined in and called to his men as they passed him by.

'Get some grub and some drinks,' he advised, 'and be ready to ride at ten minutes' notice. We may have to go back to that gully to run those Mexes out. I'll see you later. I need to send a wire to the army and get some troopers heading out to back up Captain Moran.'

The Rangers needed no urging, and

headed for the livery barn. Manning rode along the street to the telegraph office. The telegraph operator was in the act of closing for the night, but the wire was sent and Manning, satisfied that he had done all that was possible in the name of duty, made an effort to relax. He took his horse to the livery barn, attended to its needs, and then went to look for his men. He was eating a meal in the local saloon when an army officer entered, looked around, and then made his way to Manning's table.

'Captain Manning?' He paused until Manning nodded. 'I'm Lieutenant Anderson, Company B, First US cavalry. I've seen the wire you sent to army headquarters, and wired for further orders. I've been ordered to report to Captain Moran. Can you pinpoint his last position? I've got a patrol of cavalry with me and we'll be heading out in fifteen minutes.'

'Moran will be relieved to see you, Lieutenant,' Manning replied. 'I guess you know this area, huh?'

'Sure thing,' Lieutenant Anderson nodded. He was a big man with large features, steady brown eyes and a cheerful smile. His blue uniform was streaked with dust. He looked tired, but was ready to ride through the night to reach Moran. Manning gave concise directions to the gully where the stolen supplies were located. Anderson nodded and turned to depart, but Manning called him back.

'Lieutenant, I don't wanta sound like I'm trying to tell you your job, but Gonzalez is pulling out all the stops to get those stolen supplies, and I reckon he'll have a small army on this side of the river. You'll need more than a patrol of cavalry to chase him back across the Big Muddy.'

'I'm ahead of you, Captain.' Anderson grinned. 'I've already asked headquarters for reinforcements to head directly to the trouble spot.' He lifted a hand in farewell and departed quickly.

Manning was thoughtful as he

continued with his meal. He cast his mind back over the events of the past day and was satisfied that he had done everything possible. Now it was time to relax. He would wire his headquarters in the morning for further orders. He drank some beer and left the saloon to check on his men. What had occurred along the Mexican border was all in a day's work, and his mind was at ease.

★ ★ ★

When Gonzalez discovered that Moran had decamped he sent three of his men to track him down before turning his attention to the buried supplies in the gully. His voice was harsh as he shouted orders to his waiting men, and watched intently as they began shifting the rocks which the explosion had brought down into the gully. Twenty men pulled and tugged at the rocks, heaving them aside, and they worked furiously under Gonzalez's steady gaze.

It took them more than two hours to

uncover the first of the crates lying under the rocks. Gonzalez hurried forward when a shout rang out, and ordered the men to work harder. He was concerned about the *gringo* who had escaped, and feared that the US cavalry might be on its way to the gully. But his scouts were out, and there had been no reports of American military activity in the area.

The Mexicans maintained their efforts and eventually uncovered the crates containing the new rifles. Some of the boxes were broken open and the enclosed weapons, covered in grease, were displayed. Gonzalez examined one and his dark eyes glittered. He called to one of his trusted men.

'Ramos, we need a couple of wagons to move these supplies. Don't waste any time. Send some men back across the river to fetch wagons. We'll have all these supplies uncovered by the time you get back. We must be out of here before the US army shows up.'

'Where are the wagons that were

used to bring the supplies here?' Ramos asked.

'If you can find them, and the horses, you will save a lot of time,' Gonzalez replied. 'See what you can do, but remember that we must be away before the sun rises tomorrow.'

Ramos nodded and called to some of the men. They mounted up and rode off, following wagon tracks. Gonzalez urged his men to renew their efforts in moving the rocks. He set some of his men to cleaning the new rifles, and when the boxes of ammunition were discovered he equipped a patrol and sent it out to guard against a surprise attack by US cavalry.

Gonzalez was elated by his success. He had been waiting impatiently for these supplies, and now he could push ahead with his plans. He gave orders for the stores to be stacked in the entrance to the gully, and stood watching the stack grow as the work of recovering the crates and barrels continued.

Moran rode fast to get clear of the Mexicans shooting at him, and then circled to approach the entrance to the gully from the east. He could not leave the area, and planned to delay Gonzalez until help arrived. He left his horse in dense brush, took his rifle, and sneaked over the rough ground until he could see the mouth of the gully. He lay in cover and watched the stack of supplies growing rapidly as the Mexicans continued to unearth the crates and barrels he had buried with the explosion. He frowned when he saw the boxes containing the rifles, and considered his chances of delaying the transportation of the supplies into Mexico.

He knew Gonzalez would need wagons to shift the stores, and went back for his horse, intending to ride towards the river. He heard his horse stamping before he reached it, and dropped into cover to approach the animal warily. He was surprised to see two of the horses that had pulled one of the supply wagons standing with his mount, and quickly checked his surroundings for trouble. He saw nothing suspicious, and emerged from cover to approach his horse, his pistol cocked and ready in his right hand. He left the two wagon horses standing and swung into his saddle, intending to ride towards the river. If he could intercept the wagons Gonzalez must have sent for then he could delay the removal of the supplies. He was certain that military help for him would be on its way now, and he had no intention of waiting until it arrived.

He heard the sound of a wagon to his right as he headed away from the gully and rode into cover, dismounted and left his horse. The wagon approached quickly — one of the two used by the deserters — its wheels throwing up dust, and he cocked his .45 when he saw two Mexicans on the driving seat. In the background he spotted two more Mexicans riding towards the spot where he had left the other two wagon horses.

Moran stepped out of cover to confront the wagon when it drew within range. The driver hauled on the reins while his companion pulled a pistol from his belt. Moran fired quickly and the Mexican lifting his gun jerked back and then pitched sideways off the high seat. The driver quickly raised his hands. Moran knew he could not afford to take a prisoner. He half turned away from the wagon, and then swung back quickly to see the Mexican reaching for his holstered pistol. Moran shot him in the chest before turning away to run back to where he had left his horse.

He swung into his saddle and headed for the spot where he had left the other horses. Two Mexicans were leading the animals away to the left. Moran glimpsed the second wagon standing in the background. He spurred his horse and bore down on the Mexicans. Both men were holding pistols, and they twisted in their saddles to face him, their guns levelling. Moran triggered his Colt and gun smoke blew back into his face. The nearest Mexican took a slug and fell forward over the neck of his mount before sliding sideways and falling out of his saddle.

The second Mexican dived out of his saddle. His horse wheeled away, scared by the shooting. Moran hauled on his reins and brought his mount to a halt. The Mexican popped up out of the brush, his gun flaming, and Moran took evasive action. He kicked his feet out of his stirrups and jumped down from his horse to land heavily on his feet, jarring his body. He ducked behind the animal, dropped to the ground, and dived under its belly. The horse lunged sideways away from him, and Moran straightened, his gun lifting. The Mexican was almost within an arm's length, a pistol in his right hand and a knife in the other. The gun was evidently empty for the Mexican did not try to use it.

Moran jerked his pistol towards the Mexican. The man threw his pistol and it struck Moran's gun. The weapon exploded; the bullet ricocheted from a rock to his right. Moran dropped his gun and had no time to regain it. The Mexican was almost upon him, and sunlight glinted on the naked blade in his left hand. Moran threw up his right arm to block the knife thrust. The Mexican's wrist thudded against Moran's forearm. Moran set his feet and grabbed at the Mexican's wrist. He secured a hold and threw his weight and strength into his right arm. His fingers gripped the Mexican's wrist and twisted the arm as he bore down on it. He stamped on the Mexican's left foot, and then brought up his knee to thud into the man's groin.

The Mexican was tall and heavily built, although he was smaller than Moran. He gasped for breath and sweat ran down his swarthy features. He grunted like an animal when Moran's knee struck him, and tried to twist away, but Moran held on to his wrist and exerted more pressure. The Mexican smashed his head forward, trying to butt Moran, who tilted his head to the left. The Mexican's forehead struck Moran on the cheekbone. Moran pulled back, dragging his adversary with him. The Mexican threw himself backwards and dropped on to his back. Moran went with him, intent on retaining his hold on the man's wrist. They rolled on the rough ground, Moran ensuring that the knife was well clear of his body.

Moran landed on top of the Mexican and pinned him down as he reached across with his left hand to secure a double-handed grip on the Mexican's wrist. He forced the man's arm down and began to push the knife towards the Mexican. The man became desperate as the point of the blade edged towards his left side. He kicked and struggled, and arched his body in an attempt to dislodge Moran. Then he opened his hand and dropped the knife.

'Don't kill me, *señor*,' he gasped. 'I am unarmed now.'

Moran snatched up the knife and pushed himself to his feet. The Mexican remained motionless, gasping for breath and looking up at Moran with fear in his dark eyes. Moran backed off and glanced around for his pistol. He saw it and grabbed it, cocking it as he covered the Mexican.

'You just got lucky,' Moran observed. He moved in again and crashed the barrel of the .45 against the man's head.

The Mexican groaned and relaxed. Moran turned away and went back to his horse. He mounted and rode out fast to lose himself in the brush.

★　★　★

Aguilar made it across the river but his strength was waning and he was beginning to feel feverish and unsteady. His eyesight was playing tricks, fading and distorting for moments at a time. But he was back on Mexican soil, and he pushed his horse into a lope, clinging to its black mane to retain his seat. Stabs of pain were prominent in his chest and he could feel blood dribbling down his side. He needed to get off the main trail, for more of Gonzalez's men would be heading towards the gully on the American side of the river and he was aware that if he was confronted his chances of survival would be nil.

He eased to one side of the trail and headed for the nearest village. He needed to send a man to contact Sanchez, and then he would be at liberty to consult a medico. When he heard riders approaching from the south he rode into cover and remained in his saddle, sprawled over the neck of his horse, aware that if he dismounted he might not be able to summon the strength to climb back into leather. He gripped his pistol in his right hand and prepared to sell his life dearly. Five riders passed quickly along the trail, heading for the river. He recognized them as Gonzalez's men, for he had ridden with them for years until the break between Gonzalez and Sanchez had made them enemies.

When they had gone he continued, and a mile along the trail he rode into a village he knew well. There were just two rows of single-storey adobe dwellings, drab and dilapidated. The street was practically deserted, and he reined up in front of the only cantina and slid wearily out of his saddle. For a moment he clung to the horse while his gaze wavered and the street seemed to undulate. His legs were trembling uncontrollably, but he made an effort and hitched the horse before staggering into the shade of the squat building.

The interior of the cantina was gloomy. Several peons were seated at rough tables, and a big, fleshy Mexican in shirt sleeves was standing motionless behind the bar, his arms folded across a more than ample stomach that was covered by a dirty, stained apron. Aquilar weaved across to the bar, concentrating on his legs, which seemed to have developed a will of their own. He sprawled against the bar and leaned his elbows on it for support. The bartender looked at him for a moment, and then cleared his throat.

'It looks like you've made one raid too many, Aguilar,' he said, reaching for a bottle of tequila and a glass.

'Is Carlos around, Martinez?' Aguilar snatched up the glass when it was placed before him and gulped down the fiery liquid. 'I need to send a message to Sanchez.'

'If the message is to do with those Yankee guns Gonzalez is after then you can forget it,' Martinez growled in a rasping tone. 'Gonzalez has got us pegged down tight, and he'll shoot anyone who goes against him.'

'You want to see him as president?' Aquilar groaned as his right elbow slipped off the bar and his injured ribs thudded against it. 'Sanchez is the man for every right-thinking Mexican. If Gonzalez keeps pushing for a revolution there'll be a *rurale* skulking behind every bush along the border, and we'll be out of business. Find someone to go for Sanchez.'

'What is the message?' Martinez scratched his left armpit.

'The guns were taken back from the soldiers who stole them by a Yankee army officer. He told me he had orders to hand the supplies over to Sanchez.'

'Gonzalez has fifty men with him to guard those supplies.' Martinez shook his head emphatically. 'I saw them ride through some time ago. You'd better go for Sanchez yourself. No one around here will take a chance of falling foul of Gonzalez.'

'I am in no condition to ride.' Aguilar clutched at the bar for support. He could feel his senses receding. His legs were losing their strength, trembling convulsively. 'Give me another drink.'

'You haven't paid for the first one yet.' Martinez held out a hand.

Aguilar fumbled in a pocket, produced a peso, and threw it on the bar. Martinez poured him another drink.

Aguilar lifted the glass to his lips, swallowed half its contents, and then slid down the front of the bar and dropped to the floor. Martinez came around the bar and gazed at him. He bent and placed a hand over Aguilar's heart, found it beating, and straightened.

'Hey, Maria, get out here pronto,' he called, and a short, buxom woman appeared from an inner room. 'Go fetch the medico. No. Wait.' He turned to look at the men seated at the tables. 'Emilio, you and two others take Aguilar to the doctor. Don't let any of Gonzalez's men see you.'

Three men arose reluctantly and came to lift Aguilar. They carried him out the back door. Martinez watched them go before turning to his wife.

'Go to Carlos Morales and tell him Aguilar was here with a message. Sanchez has to be told that a Yankee army officer said the stolen supplies are for him, not Gonzalez. Tell Sanchez to come ready to fight. Gonzalez has fifty men to guard the supplies.'

Maria turned obediently and departed. Martinez grimaced and poured himself a drink. He and most of the men in the village were secretly for Sanchez . . .

★ ★ ★

Rosita sighed with relief when she spotted the lights of her aunt's ranch. She reined in and Wade, the Ranger accompanying her, glanced questioningly at her.

'I can make it on my own from here,' Rosita said.

'You heared what Cap'n Manning told me,' Wade replied. 'I have to see you safely to your aunt, which means I take you right into the ranch.'

'You should be in Del Rio right now, with the rest of the Rangers.'

'Don't I know it!' Wade grimaced. 'But duty comes first. I'll drop you off and then ride for Del Rio.'

Rosita sent her horse on and rode towards the lights in the distance. She was hoping that Alfredo Gomez, her intended future husband, would be waiting for her. Minutes later they rode into the yard of the ranch, which had a six-foot adobe wall built around it in the manner of a Mexican hacienda. A shadowy figure appeared in the doorway of a barn, and lamplight glinted on a rifle he was holding. A low challenge came, accompanied by the metallic sounds of the rifle being cocked.

Rosita spoke quickly. 'I am Rosita Gonzalez,' she replied. 'Is Alfredo Gomez here?'

'He rode in earlier, but went out again when he learned that you had not arrived,' the guard replied. 'Hurry to the house. Your aunt is worried about you.'

'I guess you'll be OK now,' Wade said. 'I'll make tracks for Del Rio.'

'Thank you for your help,' Rosita told him, and watched him ride off.

She dismounted, turned the horse over to the guard, and hurried across to the ranch house. A figure arose from a rocking chair set in the deep shadows of the porch, and a soft feminine voice called anxiously.

'Is that you, Rosita?'

'Yes, Aunt Perdita,' she replied. 'Why didn't you keep Alfredo here? Pedro Sanchez sent men to take me back, and there was much trouble on the trail.'

'So Alfredo said. That is why he rode out to look for you. Whatever possessed you to ride alone? Your father will stop at nothing to prevent your marriage to Alfredo. But come inside. You must be exhausted after your journey. We can talk later.

They entered the house, and Rosita looked critically at her aunt. Perdita Ruiz was middle-aged, tall and slim, dressed in black silk. She had been widowed for six years, and the strain of running a big ranch showed in her face. Wisps of grey laced her black hair. She embraced Rosita warmly.

'I hope I won't make trouble for you by coming here, Aunt,' Rosita said. 'But I had no one else to turn to. I couldn't stay with Father any longer. He kept me a prisoner at home, and was holding Alfredo against his will. I escaped to come here, and Father sent men to take me back. Four men almost took me on the trail just this side of the river. They turned out to be Sanchez's men; he wants to use me to put pressure on Father to stop the revolution that is being planned.'

'Your father knows better than to come here,' Perdita said firmly. 'I know too much about that brother of mine, and I wouldn't hesitate to inform the Texas Rangers of his presence if he did arrive. There is a price on his head on this side of the border.'

'And if men should come to take me back?' Rosita queried.

'I have enough men on my payroll to handle any trouble that might blow this way from Mexico. Don't worry your head about it, Rosita. You are here now, and you are safe.'

'I wish Alfredo hadn't gone looking for me,' Rosita said worriedly. 'Father said he would kill Alfredo if he didn't obey orders and stay away from me.'

'Why is your father so set against him?'

'Because Alfredo's father won't join him in the new revolution, and Alfredo has said he is against fighting the present government.'

'Let us forget about politics now. Come, I'll show you to your room. You must be hungry after your long journey.'

'I couldn't bring any clothes with me,' Rosita observed. 'I had to escape only with what I am wearing.'

Perdita put an arm around Rosita's shoulder and led her across the room. They had barely reached the inner door when the heavy silence was broken by several shots being fired out in the yard. Several harsh voices shouted, and more shots were fired. Then footsteps sounded on the patio. Rosita flinched when the front door was thrust open and two men came bustling into the room. They were Mexicans, and both were holding pistols.

Rosita recognized one of them as her father's closest friend Emilio Ramos, and her heart seemed to miss a beat.

'Ramos, what are you doing here?' she demanded.

'Your life is in danger,' the man replied. 'Sanchez is out to get his hands on you, and Gonzalez has sent me to save you. I will take you home to Chihuahua.'

'You will do no such thing!' Perdita stepped protectively in front of Rosita. 'What do you mean by bursting in here? Leave at once or it will be the worse for you. My men have orders to shoot intruders on sight.'

'You are wasting your breath,' Ramos said heavily. He was past middle age, short and fleshy. His round face was sweating. He grinned, but his eyes were cold, filled with determination. 'I have my orders, and nothing will prevent me carrying them out. Don't give me any trouble, Rosita. Come with me.' He glanced at his companion, a tall, thin, young Mexican. 'Jiminez, take Rosita out to the horses and start for the border. I will cover you and stop anyone following. I'll meet up with you later.'

'I would rather die than go with you,' Rosita said through clenched teeth as Jiminez came forward eagerly.

'You will leave without Rosita,' Perdita said firmly, 'and you can tell my brother that I will do everything in my power to stop him. Now leave my house.'

Ramos shook his head. He levelled his gun and cocked it. The metallic clicks sounded menacing in the sudden silence.

'I have orders to take Rosita or suffer the consequences for failure,' Ramos said harshly, his dark eyes glinting with determination, 'and I know what that would be so I will not let anyone or anything stand in my way. If it means killing you, Señora Ruiz, then so be it. Jiminez, take Rosita out of here now.'

Jiminez shrugged and approached Rosita. Perdita put out her hands to fend him off and he seized hold of her shoulders and thrust her aside. She staggered and would have fallen if Rosita had not grasped her.

'How dare you!' Rosita shrilled in a high-pitched tone. 'Keep your hands to yourself, you oaf!'

'Take her,' Ramos rasped. 'It was time we were heading back across the river.'

Jiminez grinned and reached for Rosita. She sank her teeth into his outstretched hand and he cursed, swung his left hand, and caught her across the face with a resounding slap. Rosita staggered back a step, her right ear ringing from the blow. Perdita launched herself at Jiminez with the ferocity of a mountain lion. She snatched at the pistol holstered on his hip, dragged it clear of leather, and used both hands in an attempt to cock it.

Ramos called a warning and came forward quickly. He dropped his left hand on the barrel of the gun as Perdita brought it up into the aim and twisted it viciously out of her grasp. He thrust the weapon back into Jiminez's holster.

'Can't I trust you to do anything,' he rasped. 'Can't you handle a woman?'

Perdita threw herself at Ramos, but he held her off easily with his left hand. Jiminez, his face suffused with a dull red tinge of embarrassment, grasped Rosita and dragged her towards the door. Rosita struggled with all her strength but she was helpless in his grip. They reached the outer doorway, and Rosita paused when a tall figure stepped into view to confront them. Lamp light glinted on a levelled six-gun. Rosita gasped in shock, for the newcomer was her beloved Alfredo Gomez.

'What is going on here?' Gomez demanded. His bronzed face was taut with anger and his glinting brown eyes held an eager light as he leaned forward and struck at the hand Jiminez was using to hold Rosita. Jiminez shouted in pain and released his grip. He reached for his pistol with a deft movement. Rosita immediately grasped his gun wrist and tried to thrust his weapon off aim.

Gomez triggered a shot and gun smoke plumed from the muzzle of his pistol. Jiminez yelled in pain and twisted away. He fell to the floor and his heels drummed a deadly tattoo of death on the tiles as a trickle of blood ran from his still body. Gomez moved swiftly into the big room and covered Ramos, his right index finger trembling eagerly on his trigger.

Ramos threw down his pistol without hesitation, aware of Gomez's prowess with a gun. He raised his hand and stood regarding Gomez with an unblinking gaze.

'Don't tell me,' Gomez said harshly. 'Gonzalez wants Rosita back.'

'You should know better than to go against Gonzalez,' Ramos shrugged. 'Your days are numbered, Gomez, and you are a fool for trying to fight.'

'At the moment it is your days that are numbered,' Gomez replied. 'Get out of here, Ramos, and tell Gonzalez he is a dead man if he persists in trying to make Rosita bend to his will. She and I will be married shortly.'

'You talk big.' Ramos showed his teeth in a wide smile. 'You will regret interfering in this matter. I cannot go back to Gonzalez without Rosita.'

'You have a choice.' Gomez's voice was pitched low. 'Leave without further trouble or die where you are standing. It is up to you. I don't care which you decide.'

Ramos shrugged. 'I will leave now,' he said, 'but this is not the end of it.'

He bent to pick up his discarded pistol. Gomez stepped forward quickly and kicked the weapon away from Ramos's outstretched hand.

'You will leave without your gun,' Gomez said sharply.

'That would be a death sentence,' Ramos observed bleakly. 'There are many enemies between here and the river.'

'Which is your problem, not mine.

You have ten seconds to clear the yard before I start shooting.'

Ramos jumped into action. He hurried to the door and departed soundlessly. Rosita, watching him disappear into the shadows, was filled with fear, for she realized that his departure was not the end of the affair but merely the beginning, and she despaired of ever finding a happy outcome to her troubles.

6

Moran rode until he was well clear of the gully, and then looked around for a quiet place in which to rest up. He was exhausted, and ached in every muscle. His left thigh just above the knee was throbbing from a flesh wound. His right cheekbone was swollen and felt as if it had been broken by the headbutt he had received. There was a bullet slash across his left forearm. His head ached. He was thirsty and hungry, and weariness filled him like a deadly plague. He came upon a defile in the brush and dismounted to enter it, leading his horse. He was close to the main trail that led north, and was hopeful, as a result of Captain Manning's proposed wire to army headquarters, of relief coming down the trail in the form of a troop of US cavalry.

He off-saddled and tethered the

horse, then rummaged in his saddle-bags for cold food. He found some and after eating, washed it down with water from his canteen. He sat down to clean his pistol and rifle. His eyelids were heavy and he had trouble remaining alert. He fell asleep without being aware of his lapse of concentration, came back to his senses once to find that night had fallen, and slept again until an unnatural noise stabbed through his sleep. He opened his eyes blearily to see that daylight had returned. He looked around quickly in the early morning sunlight but saw no immediate danger.

He had been awakened by two Mexicans nearby who were talking loudly. He drew his pistol, crouched in the brush, suspecting that his position had been discovered. He understood a smattering of the Mexican language, and picked up enough from what was being said to ascertain that the two men were part of Gonzalez's faction — one wanted to give up the hunt for Moran and the other thought they should continue to search.

Moran gleaned the fact that the pair were looking for him, and he watched them intently from cover. They were sitting their mounts on the trail; two drably dressed, heavily armed men whose swarthy faces were shadowed by the wide brims of their sombreros. They were unaware of being observed by their quarry. The man who was keen to give up the search argued noisily, pointing out that no fresh tracks were visible on the trail, and when he failed to persuade his companion to quit he turned his horse to the south and spurred it back the way they had come. The other sat watching his departure for some moments before reluctantly following. Moran watched their dust settle and considered the situation.

He was aware that he could not sit around hoping for relief to appear. His duty was clear. He had to ensure that the stolen supplies reached Pedro Sanchez, therefore he had to prevent Gonzalez from stealing the shipment.

He was bound to keep the supplies on this side of the border, and that meant continuing the action against the Mexicans. He saddled up, led the horse on to the trail, and headed back towards the gully.

When he was in a position to observe the entrance to the gully where the supplies had been concealed he realized that he could do nothing to change the situation that existed. Two Mexicans were on guard in the entrance, and just inside the gully he saw both wagons, with the horses that pulled them, standing tethered nearby. Moran grimaced. So Gonzalez had recovered the wagons despite the action of yesterday! Several Mexicans were seated around a camp-fire inside the gully, and Moran found a small grain of comfort in the fact that Gonzalez had not yet succeeded in unearthing all of the supplies.

Moran realized it would be hopeless trying to attack the Mexicans — he was so greatly outnumbered — so he moved away, returned to his horse, and departed from the scene. He headed for the northern trail. His only alternative, he mused, was to look for reinforcements coming from the direction of Del Rio, and he rode fast in anticipation of finding help.

He had travelled about ten miles when he topped a rise and saw a patrol of twenty cavalrymen coming towards him. He rode into the open and waved his hat to attract their attention. The officer leading the patrol saw him and increased his pace. Moran rode fast towards him.

'I'm Captain Moran. Are you here about the stolen supplies, Lieutenant?'

'Yes, sir, I am,' Lieutenant Anderson replied, saluting smartly. 'I saw Captain Manning of the Texas Rangers in Del Rio last night and he told me about you, Captain. I sent a wire to headquarters asking for reinforcements to be sent to this spot, but I doubt if anyone will turn up before tomorrow. They have a long way to come.'

'And we have to hurry,' Moran

mused. 'There are about forty Mexicans in a gully near here, where I buried the supplies. If we move fast we'll catch them red-handed. Split your men into two groups. I'll lead one into the top of the gully while you take the rest around to the bottom entrance. We'll catch the Mexicans between us and wipe them out.'

'Yes, sir!' Eagerness sounded in Anderson's voice and his eyes brightened at the thought of impending action. He spoke to a sergeant. 'Bring the men along,' he ordered.

Moran turned his mount and started back along the trail. The patrol of cavalry followed him closely. When he reached the spot where he needed to turn off to reach the high ground above the gully he reined in and explained the situation.

'I'll take half your men and we'll ascend the high ground to enter the top of the gully, Lieutenant. You take the rest and head on along this trail until the low ground on your left peters out.

Turn left there and you'll see the lower end of the gully on your left about five hundred yards on. Enter the gully and meet us coming down from the top. The Mexicans should be between us.'

Lieutenant Anderson nodded his understanding, saluted, and led half his troop on along the trail. The sergeant and the rest of the cavalry followed Moran, who rode to the spot where he had left his horse. They dismounted, went on foot to the high ground, and ascended quickly. Moran paused at the top and they rested to regain their breath.

'We'll need to give the lieutenant time to reach the lower end of the gully, Sergeant,' Moran observed. 'We'll continue in ten minutes.'

The soldiers were seasoned campaigners. They checked their weapons and waited silently until Moran got to his feet and ran to the top entrance to the gully. They entered, bunched together in their eagerness, and the sergeant ordered them to space out. They followed Moran down to where the explosion had taken place. Moran climbed to the top of the pile of rubble blocking the gully and peered into the lower part. He clenched his teeth when he saw that all of the supplies he had buried had been dug out and removed.

He could see the rest of the gully all the way down to the lower entrance, and paused when a movement below caught his eye. He saw uniforms as the party of soldiers with Lieutenant Anderson appeared and began to advance to where he was standing.

Moran was disappointed. The Mexicans had pulled out. He hurried down to meet Anderson, who confirmed that the Mexicans had gone.

'There's no time to lose,' Moran said. 'Back to your horses, Lieutenant, and head for the river. With any luck you could catch up with the Mexicans before they can get across. They can't be far ahead. Send one of your men with the sergeant's party and they can collect our horses and follow on to the river. I'll go with you.'

Lieutenant Anderson issued orders and the sergeant returned up the gully with his group. Moran accompanied the others. They left the gully and returned to their horses. In a few moments they were mounted and Moran led them at a gallop towards the Rio Grande a few miles away.

The trail to the river twisted like a serpent through a long stretch of rocky ground. Moran urged his borrowed horse into a reckless gallop, aware only that he had to regain possession of the wagons. The cavalry followed closely. Lieutenant Anderson rode on Moran's left. They swept around a bend in the trail where a jumble of rocks blocked their view of the way ahead. When the trail straightened out, Moran saw figures ahead and drew his gun.

One of the wagons was halted with a broken back wheel, and five Mexicans stood around it, trying to effect repairs. They swung round at the sound of approaching horses, saw the soldiers, and separated quickly, diving for cover, yelling and drawing weapons.

Moran opened fire while urging his horse closer. The cavalry began shooting. The raucous blasts of their guns smashed the silence and sent echoes flying to the horizon. Slugs came back quickly from the Mexicans but the soldiers did not hesitate. They swept by the wagon, shooting rapidly, and when they turned to charge again the opposition was non-existent. All of the Mexicans were down.

The two horses hitched to the wagon were terrified by the shooting and bolted, hauling the wagon along the trail with its axle dragging in the dust. Moran rode forward, seized the bridle of the nearest horse, and halted the team. A trooper came forward to soothe the horses. Moran turned to Anderson.

'We've got to stop the other wagon reaching the river,' he rapped. 'Let's raise dust.'

Anderson told three troopers to remain with the wagon and led the rest behind Moran, who spurred his horse into a gallop and continued towards the distant river. As he neared another bend, three rifles began firing from cover at the side of the trail, and he ducked as a slug snarled in his left ear in passing. He returned fire without hesitation, aiming at gun smoke spurting up from the positions of the ambushers. The troopers followed him closely, their guns hammering, and they passed through the ambush without loss.

Moran was intent upon sighting the second wagon. He pushed on rapidly until he neared the bank of the river, and, as soon as he rode into the open area leading to the water's edge at least a dozen rifles opened fire from positions on the near bank. He swung his horse hurriedly to the left and rode into cover with the troopers following. They dismounted. Moran pulled his rifle from the saddleboot, dropped into cover with slugs crackling around him, and returned fire.

The cavalrymen quickly dropped into

firing positions and went into action. Moran could see the river crossing fifty yards ahead. His eyes glinted when he spotted a small party of Mexicans herding the second wagon through the shallow water towards the far bank. He was aware that when the wagon reached the other side of the river it would be safely in Mexico and beyond his control. He opened fire on the attendant Mexicans and they scattered. But the wagon kept moving steadily, throwing up a spray of water that glinted in the strong sunlight. Moran clenched his teeth and aimed for the horses pulling the wagon. He hated to shoot animals but had to stop the supplies.

His carefully aimed shot struck the right-hand horse in the head and it dropped into the water, its legs thrashing. The other horse panicked and tried to get away. The wagon slewed and stopped. The level of the river was no more than belly-high to the horses but the current was swift and the wagon moved slightly under its ceaseless pressure. Moran shot the second horse, killing it instantly. The bodies of both animals acted as anchors, holding the wagon immobile in mid-stream.

The volume of shooting increased considerably when the group of soldiers led by the sergeant arrived on the scene. The Mexicans stood their ground as long as possible, but they had no stomach for a protracted fight on American soil. One or two began to pull back and the rest quickly followed, sped on their way by the accurate shooting of the soldiers. The shooting died away and an uneasy silence settled over the river.

Moran watched the wagon, motionless in the river. There were no Mexicans around the vehicle but some were crowded on the far bank. Lieutenant Anderson ordered his best rifle shots to snipe at the Mexicans, and Moran felt easier when fresh shooting started compelling the Mexicans to take cover.

'We need to take possession of that wagon, Captain,' Lieutenant Anderson commented, coming to Moran's side.

'It'll be safe enough where it is until sundown,' Moran replied. 'We can keep it under our guns while we can see it, but we'll have to guard against Gonzalez sending men across the river at some other point and sneaking around to the wagon with the broken wheel. Gonzalez must be getting desperate now. He had all of the supplies in his hands, but has lost them before he could cross the river. But he won't give up the fight, and I shan't be happy until I've moved both wagons out of his reach.'

'We could start the other wagon back along the trail north if that broken wheel can be fixed,' Lieutenant Anderson observed. 'A squad could escort it, and it would be out of danger with us holding this crossing.'

'I have to hand over the two wagons to a Mexican named Sanchez, who is opposing Gonzalez,' Moran said, 'but at the moment I have no idea where he is so we must move the supplies to a safer place until I can find him. I'll go back to the other wagon and check it out.

The wagon is a military vehicle and is likely to have a spare wheel.'

'With any luck there should be re-inforcements heading this way. I'll keep this situation under control until you get back, Captain.' Anderson saluted smartly.

Moran returned the salute and went to his horse. He swung into the saddle and rode back along the trail to where the broken-down wagon was immobilized. When he reached it he found the two soldiers left behind to guard it already working to fit a replacement wheel on the axle.

'We're in luck, Captain,' one reported. 'We'll be ready to roll shortly.'

'Good.' Moran nodded. 'As soon as you are able, head back along the trail north and keep going towards Del Rio. I'll arrange for an escort to accompany you. On your way, if you see reinforcements coming, report our situation to them.'

As he was speaking, Moran realized that he had not seen Gonzalez on his white horse since returning to the gully with the cavalry, and wondered where the bandit had gone. He returned to the river, where all was quiet, and studied the far bank before conferring with Lieutenant Anderson.

'Perhaps you'll send your sergeant and four men to escort that other wagon to Del Rio,' he said. 'Gonzalez might try crossing with more men somewhere along the river and attempt to seize it.'

'I'll give Sergeant Johnson orders.' Anderson went off along the river-bank.

Moran put his horse under cover and drew his rifle. He settled down to watch the wagon in midstream. There was no activity now across the river, and he wondered how long it would take the Mexicans to regroup. But at that moment all he could do was wait . . .

* * *

In Del Rio that morning, Captain Manning awakened long before dawn. He had slept uneasily through the night, and while he cleaned his weapons he analysed his thoughts to discover what was bothering him. The answer came to him instantly — the Mexican trouble on the border. He sighed long and hard, and became aware, without hesitation, that he would have to return to the gully where he had left Captain Moran alone with two wagonloads of arms to face the overwhelming odds of Gonzalez and his bandits.

Hurrying to the restaurant on Main Street, he found one of his men already feeding his face. He sat down across from Wade and ordered breakfast. Wade pushed aside his empty plate and leaned his elbows on the table.

'I reckon we'll be going back to fight Gonzalez some more, huh, Captain?' he asked.

'I guess,' Manning replied. 'Go round up the men and tell them to be ready to ride in ten minutes.'

'I've already done that,' Wade said, getting to his feet. 'They'll be waiting at the livery barn right now, raring to go.

I'll go saddle up your bronc. We'll be ready to leave the minute you show up along the street.'

'That's what I like about you, Wade,' Manning said with a tight grin. 'I don't have to tell you a darn thing. But why didn't you say something last night? If you had, we would have been on the trail south at least an hour ago.'

'I ain't one for telling another man what he's gotta do,' Wade replied with a grin, and headed for the door.

Manning called for the waitress to hurry his breakfast along, and when it arrived he attacked it like a condemned man eating his last meal. Fifteen minutes later he walked into the telegraph office and asked for any wires addressed to Captain Moran. The operator handed him one sealed message for Moran and Manning stuffed it into the breast pocket of his jacket. He hurried to the stable, greeted his men, swung into his saddle, and led the four of them out to the trail. They headed south in a cloud of dust.

Aguilar was carried from the cantina to the local doctor's house. When he regained consciousness he was lying on a couch, and the wound in his chest had obviously been treated because he was now heavily bandaged. It took him some moments to piece together what had happened, then he sat up, grunting in pain. He got to his feet with difficulty. He was in a small room which he knew to be the doctor's office and he opened the door to peer out into a long passage. He called the doctor's name and a door along the passage opened. Doctor Lopez appeared.

'What are you doing on your feet?' the medico demanded.

'I am well enough to stand so I have to go about my business,' Aguilar said. He walked unsteadily to the front door with Lopez in close attendance.

'Try and rest up as much as possible,' Lopez said. 'You have a broken rib. I have strapped it tightly, but you should not move unduly until it has knitted together.'

'I can rest when I get old,' Aguilar responded.

'If you don't rest now you may not live to see old age,' Lopez replied tartly.

Aguilar ignored him and departed. His horse was still standing tethered in front of the cantina. He went to it and climbed laboriously into the saddle, grunting in pain as he did so. He sat motionless, considering his next move, and looked up when Martinez appeared in the doorway of the cantina.

'I've sent my wife to pass on your message,' Martinez said. 'You owe me for that, Aguilar.'

'I'm sure Sanchez will reward you when he hears of your kind act.' Aguilar grinned despite his pain. 'If Sanchez comes by this way be sure to tell him that I have gone to carry out his orders.'

'What orders would they be?'

'That is between Sanchez and me.' Aguilar winked and turned his horse to ride back to the river. He had some unfinished business with Rosita Gonzalez, and he knew where she was and how to reach her.

He heard shooting coming from the direction of the river and slowed his pace as he neared the waterway, aware of the great number of men Gonzalez had taken with him to collect the two wagons. Not wishing to be confronted by any of Gonzalez's men, he angled away from the trail and crossed the border north of the main crossing. He looked downstream and saw the stranded wagon in midstream with its two-horse team dead in the water. Nodding, he continued on his way, no longer concerned with the fate of the wagons and their contents. If Sanchez wanted the supplies then he would have to take the steps necessary to obtain them.

When he reached the main trail and turned north for Del Rio, Aguilar heard hoofs and wagon wheels to his rear, and quickened his pace until he drew well ahead. He reined in beyond a rise and watched his back trail until a wagon appeared. Two soldiers were on the driving seat, and a squad of five cavalrymen was escorting it. Not wanting to fall behind the wagon, he rode on, making an effort to pull ahead. He felt weak. His body was racked with pain, and he realized he was getting feverish. The sun seemed more than usually bright and he was having difficulty focusing his eyes on surrounding objects. Several times, as he progressed, he swayed in the saddle, and once almost lost consciousness, but he stuck to his task and continued.

His condition worsened in the next hour and his senses wavered as his strength failed. He had to cling to his saddle while his horse cantered along the trail, and time passed in a nightmarish daze. He seemed to be riding through a wilderness in which he was the only living thing. His alertness faded and he was no longer fully aware of his surroundings. His eyes lost their long range and he had to blink furiously at times to keep them open. He was not aware of falling from his horse, and lost consciousness when he hit the ground in the middle of the trail that seemed to have been leading him nowhere.

Aguilar lay for an hour before a hand grasped his shoulder and shook him back to consciousness. He opened his eyes and narrowed them against the glare of the brassy sun. The pale oval of a face was bent over him and he blinked. His eyes focused on the face and he was astonished when he recognized Rosita Gonzalez.

'Aguilar,' she said. 'What are you doing here in this sad condition? Where is Captain Moran?'

'The *gringo* has soldiers with him,' Aguilar muttered. 'They have taken one of the supply wagons from Gonzalez, and the other is stranded in the middle of the Rio Grande. Take me to Sanchez, I beg you.'

'So he can use me as a lever against my father?' Rosita laughed harshly. 'What are you doing on the trail to Del Rio? You're after me again, aren't you? How did you get shot?'

'You have so many questions!'

Aguilar shook his head. His forehead was beaded with sweat and it ran down his face in tiny rivulets. 'Help me to get back across the border.'

Rosita's face faded from his sight and was replaced by the harsh countenance of Alfredo Gomez, who seized hold of Aguilar's bloodied shirt and shook him roughly,

'You dog, Aguilar! Rosita told me how you grabbed her to take her to Sanchez as a hostage against Gonzalez. I'm tempted to end your miserable life here and now. You're a renegade. You left Gonzalez when Sanchez broke away, and you stooped low to do Sanchez's bidding. What are you doing on this side of the border? If I thought you were chasing after Rosita again I wouldn't hesitate to put a bullet through your black heart.'

Before Aguilar could protest, Gomez swung away and peered along the trail. Aguilar tried to push himself into a sitting position but failed, and he slumped on the ground. The grating of wagon wheels sounded, and then a harsh North American voice called out sharply.

'What's going on here?' Sergeant Johnson demanded.

'We found this man lying here, Sergeant,' Rosita said. 'He had fallen from his horse.'

'Who are you and where have you come from?'

'We are Rosita Gonzalez and Alfredo Gomez. We are going back to Mexico after visiting my aunt's ranch near Del Rio.'

'And who is the man on the ground?' Johnson asked. 'If he's been shot then he must have taken part in the action we are fighting. Does he ride with Gonzalez?'

'His name is Aguilar. He rides for Pedro Sanchez across the border,' Rosita replied, and added: 'He is against Gonzalez.'

'Anyone against Gonzalez must be for us.' Sergeant Johnson dismounted and bent over Aguilar. 'Who bandaged him?' he demanded.

'We don't know,' Gomez said.

'If you are going back to Mexico then take him with you,' Johnson suggested.

'Yes.' Rosita spoke hesitantly. 'We will do that. There is a village just across the river — we'll leave him there.'

Johnson nodded. He went back to his horse and swung into the saddle. The wagon carrying supplies had stopped in the background.

'There's shooting trouble at the crossing south of here,' Johnson said. 'You'd do well to stay away from it.' He tipped his hat to Rosita and signalled for the wagon to continue.

Aguilar grunted in pain as he forced himself into a sitting position. 'Where are you taking that wagon?' he called to Sergeant Johnson.

'It's bound for Del Rio.'

'But Captain Moran said all the supplies are to go to Pedro Sanchez, and he sent me across the border to contact Sanchez.'

'I heard the captain mention that,' Sergeant Johnson nodded. 'But it ain't my business. I got my orders to take this wagon to Del Rio, where it'll be safe. If you were sent across the border to contact Sanchez, then what are you doing here?'

'I sent a message to Sanchez. He will turn up soon.'

'When he does, this wagon will be brought back from Del Rio.' Johnson gigged his mount and moved on, signalling to the driver of the wagon to continue.

'Do you want to go with us back across the border, Aguilar?' Rosita asked.

'Just get me to the village on the other side of the main crossing and I'll wait there for Sanchez to show up,' he replied.

Gomez helped Aguilar into his saddle and they left the trail to head for the river. They crossed upstream from the main crossing, and saw the stranded wagon in midstream. There was no activity around the wagon, although figures could be seen on either bank.

'It looks like a Mexican stand-off,'

Gomez remarked. 'Gonzalez dare not attack the Yankee soldiers.'

'I don't want to run the risk of facing my father at this time,' Rosita said.

'He won't get the chance to send you back home,' Gomez responded firmly.

'I don't want you to fight him, Alfredo, because whatever the outcome I would be the loser. I don't want to see my father dead, and I also lose if he kills you.'

'I would not kill him,' Gomez insisted.

'You would have to kill him to stop him,' she replied. She turned to Aguilar, who was sitting slumped in his saddle. 'You should be able to reach the village unaided from here,' she told him. 'I have changed my mind. We are turning back.'

'Don't let me see your ugly face again,' Gomez warned Aguilar. 'The next time we meet I will kill you.'

Aguilar groaned as he straightened himself in his saddle. He touched spurs to the flanks of his horse and sent the animal forward at a walk, swaying in the saddle as they traversed the rough ground. He headed for the distant village, and each step his horse took was a separate nightmare. Rosita watched his progress until Gomez touched her arm.

'It is time to go,' he said gently. 'The question is, where do we ride? Shall we head for Chihuahua or go to my father's hacienda? Whatever we do, we must ensure that Gonzalez cannot get his hands on either of us.'

'We can never be safe in Mexico,' Rosita replied. 'I think I had better go back to my Aunt Perdita. I don't want to take any trouble to her, but she is family, and will take care of me. You will stay with me, Alfredo. I want to be able to keep an eye on you after this. Bad things are about to happen and we must stay out of harm's way. But first, I want to see that *gringo* captain who is fighting my father.'

Gomez nodded reluctantly. They turned, went back across the river, and rode towards the main crossing where the action was taking place.

7

Gonzalez left the two wagons on the American side of the border as soon as they had set out on the trail to the river. He was satisfied that they were safely in his possession, with almost fifty of his men escorting them. He had other important business to handle, and was looking forward to locating Pedro Sanchez, his one-time friend and henchman but now his most bitter rival. He was hoping he could change Sanchez's one-track mind and persuade him to back the revolution. If he failed to accomplish that aim then he would have no recourse but to eliminate Sanchez.

He rode across the river ahead of the wagons, accompanied by a five-man bodyguard, and made for the nearest village. He had no idea where Sanchez was at that moment, but he was aware that the inhabitants of the village, led and bullied by Martinez, the owner of the cantina, were adherents of Sanchez. He paused on the outskirts of the village and instructed three of his men to guard against attack, then rode on with two men and dismounted outside the cantina. He warned his remaining two men to be on their guard. His spiked rowels tinkled as he tramped through the dust and entered the single-storey adobe building.

Martinez was seated at a table, eating his breakfast. He looked up at Gonzalez's entrance, and sprang to his feet when he recognized his early morning visitor.

'Welcome to my humble cantina, Señor Gonzalez,' he greeted ingratiatingly. 'This is a pleasant surprise. Would you like some breakfast?'

'You are a poor liar, Martinez,' Gonzalez grimaced distastefully. 'You hate me, like the rest of the miserable dogs in this village. Sanchez owns you body and soul. What do you see in that bandit? He can do nothing for you and your kind. So why do you hate me? I have nothing but your best interests at heart. I am planning the revolution to help people like you, and yet you repay me with treachery. You would put me in my grave without compunction, if you dared risk your life attempting it. Where is Sanchez? I need to talk to him.'

'I do not know his whereabouts.' Martinez chewed a mouthful of food, tried to swallow, and failed when his throat constricted convulsively. 'Señor Sanchez does not inform me of his whereabouts. He has so many enemies intent on killing him.'

'You will tell me what I want to know or you will be dead before that mouthful of food you are chewing can reach your stomach. Do not waste my time for I have important things to do today.'

'I am sorry I cannot be of help.' Martinez gulped at the food in his mouth but could not swallow it. He made a second effort, almost choked, and spat it on the floor. 'Sanchez has not been seen around here in many days. I think he is in another part of the country.'

'I can get information from anyone in the village.' Gonzalez drew his pistol and cocked it. 'But if I have to do that I will kill you first for wasting my time. What are you waiting for? Do you want to die?'

'Please! Have mercy! I would tell you willingly if I knew Sanchez's movements, but I am speaking the truth. I do not know where he is.' Martinez pressed his hands together as if in prayer. 'I am the only man in this village who believes in you, and I will do anything to help.'

Gonzalez cocked his pistol and aimed it at Martinez.

'You are standing on the brink of hell, *amigo*,' he said gently. 'In five seconds I will push you over the edge by splattering the few brains you possess over that wall behind you. You don't have time to consider; five seconds stand between you and death.'

Gonzalez began to count but paused when one of his men out front stepped into the doorway at his back.

'There's a party of four riders entering the village,' the man reported.

Gonzalez turned swiftly and hurried to the door. He peered along the street and saw the approaching riders.

'I just remembered: Sanchez is due to come here today,' Martinez called hurriedly.

'It is my old friend Sanchez,' Gonzalez observed. 'Wait outside for him, Ignacio, and send him in when he arrives. Tell him I am here waiting to see him and need to talk to him.'

The man nodded and moved out to cover the doorway. Gonzalez holstered his pistol and walked to the rear of the cantina. He sat on the chair Martinez had vacated and motioned for the inn keeper to join him. Martinez dropped reluctantly into the nearest chair.

'Don't sit between me and the door,' Gonzalez rapped, and Martinez hurriedly switched to another chair. 'Keep your mouth shut when Sanchez comes in.' Gonzalez leaned back in his seat and kept his right hand close to his holstered gun.

Hoofs sounded clearly outside the cantina. The mutter of unintelligible voices echoed in the open doorway. Boots thudded in the dust as men dismounted from their horses. Gonzalez recognized the voice of Pedro Sanchez. The doorway darkened as a figure crossed the threshold. Gonzalez smiled easily, and kept his lips frozen in a fixed grin. He studied the short, grossly large figure that entered the cantina and paused on the threshold.

'Sanchez, *mi amigo*,' Gonzalez greeted, friendliness in his tone. 'I am pleased to see you. I was asking about your whereabouts of our good friend Martinez in the hope of seeing you today, and it is fate that you have appeared so readily.'

'It had nothing to do with fate,' Sanchez replied in a husky voice. 'I had word that there was great activity across the border and assumed that your shipment of supplies had arrived. But there has been much shooting so I came to see for myself what is happening. As I came into the village someone shouted that you were fighting soldiers across the river, and if that is true then you are facing disaster.'

Sanchez grinned then, as if a disaster for Gonzalez was just what he wanted. He was short; his width almost the same as his height. His fleshy face was greasy, his forehead covered in sweat. His unblinking eyes had a piercing quality that showed no emotion. Two cartridge belts adorned his body, crossing from his shoulders to his bulging waistline. He was drably clothed in badly worn attire. A black sombrero shadowed his ugly face. Gleaming spurs were strapped on his boots, which were run down at the heels; dusty and cracked. He was accustomed to living rough, and it showed in every dusty line of his appearance.

'I am quite pleased with the way my enterprise is progressing,' Gonzalez replied. 'I have two wagons of supplies due to cross the river within the hour. That is why I want to talk to you. I need you on my side, amigo. Together we can succeed in this venture. How can you refuse to join me when there is so much at stake? When we have gained power we shall do all the things we have talked of through the years. We shall fulfil our destiny and free the little people from the yoke of poverty. This we have talked about around countless camp-fires, but now the time has come for action you are no longer of the same mind.'

'Because I feel strongly that you have over-stretched yourself this time. The people will not rise; they are sick of bloodshed. We helped them more when we were plying the trade we were born to. No one needs a revolution. We want life to stay as it is. A revolt will bring the army into the area, and that is a situation to be avoided at all costs. Change your mind about the revolution, Fernando, and I will rejoin you, but if you persist in your foolhardiness then I can do no other but oppose you.'

'If that is your attitude then we have nothing more to discuss.' Gonzalez edged his hand closer to his holstered pistol, his smile remaining on his thin lips.

Sanchez lifted his left hand casually and cuffed sweat from his brow. His dark eyes remained unblinking. His sturdy legs were braced as if he planned some kind of action but he was thinking about his withdrawal from the cantina. He knew Gonzalez intimately and suspected that, having rejected the peace offer, he would not be allowed to leave unmolested.

A slight disturbance outside the door attracted the attention of both Gonzalez and Sanchez. Gonzalez palmed his pistol and pointed it at the door. Sanchez lifted his right hand to his right ear and reached for the haft of the knife he wore in a scabbard between his shoulder blades. A shadow darkened the doorway and one of Gonzalez's two men peered inside.

'Tomas Aguilar has just ridden up,' he reported. 'He's been shot. Can I bring him in?'

'I have been expecting Aguilar,' Sanchez said.

'He is a dog,' Gonzalez observed. 'Bring him, Ignacio, and I will shoot him as he deserves.'

They waited until Aguilar was helped, half-senseless and dragging his feet, into the cantina. His eyes were closed. He leaned heavily on the two men supporting him. They dumped him on a chair and withdrew. Gonzalez lifted his pistol and aimed at Aguilar's chest but Sanchez stepped forward and covered Aguilar with his own blocky figure.

'He has been on a job for me,' Sanchez said, 'and I need to know what he has accomplished.'

'I'll give you two minutes,' Gonzalez said firmly, 'and then I will shoot him. I have heard that Aguilar tried to kidnap my daughter, and it was said that you intended holding her to use as a lever against me.'

'That is not true.' Sanchez glared at Gonzalez. 'Everyone knows you cannot be held to ransom, not even with your daughter's life. It is well known that you would murder your grandmother if there was profit in it.'

Gonzalez laughed. 'I suspect there is some truth in what you say. You have one minute left.'

'Aguilar!' Sanchez bent over the semi-conscious man and shook him roughly. 'Open your eyes, *amigo*, and answer me.'

Aguilar's eyes flickered but did not open. Sanchez shook him again.

'Pay attention, Aguilar. How did you get shot? Where have you been for two days?'

Aguilar groaned and stirred. His eyes opened, and when he looked up at Sanchez there was no sign of intelligence in his gaze. Sanchez shook him again, a little more roughly. Aguilar's head rolled on his neck. He reached up with his right hand and grasped Sanchez's hand. Sanchez looked round at the motionless Martinez.

'Bring some tequila, quickly,' he rapped.

Martinez looked at Gonzalez for permission. Gonzalez nodded. Martinez went behind the bar, tipped a bottle over a glass and filled it, and then took the glass to Sanchez. Aguilar gulped down the contents greedily when the glass was put to his lips. He swallowed noisily and presently became more animated. He managed to smile at Sanchez, and tried to sit up.

'Sanchez, what are you doing here?' Aguilar demanded. 'You've saved me the trouble of looking for you. I have much to tell you.'

'Gonzalez is here,' Sanchez cut in.

Aguilar's expression changed and fear seeped into his eyes as he looked around. He uttered a gasp of despair when he saw Gonzalez seated at the nearby table — the last time they had met Gonzalez had threatened to shoot him at their next meeting. He flinched when he noted Gonzalez's pistol pointing in his direction.

'So tell us what bad things you have been doing for Sanchez,' Gonzalez said, 'and if you admit that you've been trying to capture my daughter I will shoot you. Also, if you lie and deny it I will shoot you. I am kept well informed of everything that happens in this part of Mexico, as you know. So speak up, *amigo*, and then I can squeeze my trigger.'

'I have nothing to say,' Aguilar replied.

'And I will shoot you if you say nothing at all.' Gonzalez smiled. His eyes glinted. 'So where does that leave you? It looks as if you have run out of options.'

'Rosita is safe in the company of Alfredo Gomez,' Aguilar said. 'I saw them this morning. They were heading for the Ruiz ranch near Del Rio.'

'Gomez is another I shall kill when I catch up with him,' Gonzalez said. 'He still thinks he can marry my daughter without my permission. But Rosita will come back to me when she realizes where she will be better off.'

'Your supplies have been stolen,' Aguilar said heavily. 'While you are sitting here, one wagon is heading for

Del Rio, escorted by Yankee soldiers, and the other is stranded in the middle of the river with its horses dead in the water. Many soldiers are covering it from the far bank while your men are skulking in the bushes on this side.'

'You lie!' Gonzalez cocked his pistol and raised it to aim at Aguilar. 'Whenever you open your mouth a lie comes out.'

'It would be easy to check what I say,' Aguilar said. 'Send a man to the river.'

A silence developed in which Gonzalez gazed at Aguilar while he considered.

'You swear to me that what you say is the truth?' Gonzalez demanded at length.

'I swear it on my life!' Aguilar nodded emphatically.

'Ignacio, show your face.' Gonzalez got to his feet and walked a couple of paces towards the door. One of his men entered the cantina and paused on the threshold. Gonzalez continued: 'Ride to the river, Ignacio, and find out what is keeping the two wagons. They should be on this side of the border now.'

Ignacio hurried out. A moment later they heard the sound of hoofs departing rapidly.

'I do not like your joke,' Gonzalez said, returning to his seat. He leaned back, lifted his right leg over the arm of his chair, and swung it to and fro, his spur tapping insistently against a leg of the chair, the insistent sound seeming to echo menacingly around the room.

'I was not joking.' Aguilar lifted a limp hand and wiped sweat from his brow.

Gonzalez took a thin cigar from his breast pocket, lighted it, and puffed hard. His shrewd brown eyes narrowed as blue smoke curled around his swarthy face. He eased forward the hammer of his pistol and then cocked the weapon again.

'Aguilar, you used to be my faithful friend,' Gonzalez observed, 'until you got big ideas, that is. You left me for Sanchez, who does not know his own mind, and you do his bidding like the dog you are, hoping to get better scraps from his table than you got from mine. Have you not discovered yet that you are worse off now than you ever were with me?' He paused and the ensuing silence was heavy and ominous. 'Evidently you have not! My faithful Aguilar has not seen the error of his ways, and I am bound to make an example of him as a warning to others of my men who may be feeling that they should follow you along the wrong trail.'

'It was you who took the wrong trail,' Aguilar said in a low tone. 'You talked up the revolution when everyone knows the old ways are the best.'

'My loyal Aguilar!' Gonzalez shook his head. 'You yap like a puppy going around in circles chasing its own tail, and all you do is repeat the nonsense our friend Sanchez spouts. I would be doing you a great favour if I put you out of your misery. You have forgotten that your duty in life is to be faithful to me. But you oppose me, and I do not like it.

I do not like it one little bit.'

Aguilar blinked rapidly. He recognized the tone in Gonzalez's voice and became afraid. His breathing quickened. He forgot the pain of his wound as a thread of desperation filtered through his mind.

'I have always been faithful to you,' he said forcefully, 'even though I have turned away from you.'

'But I can no longer trust you.' Gonzalez shook his head and his bottom lip thrust forward. His eyes took on a baleful glitter. 'You would still do anything for me, yes?'

Aguilar nodded emphatically. His narrowed eyes were staring at the black muzzle of Gonzalez's pistol, which was pointed unerringly at his chest. He nodded again and his lips moved silently, as if in prayer. He straightened in his seat.

'I would do anything for you, Gonzalez.' He pressed the palms of his hands together in front of his lips, as if about to pray.

'Ha! Do you hear that, Sanchez? Aguilar has turned his coat again. How could you ever rely on him?'

'I have been thinking this past month that I would like to return to you, Gonzalez,' Aguilar said nervously. 'It dawned on me that we should all stick together. We cannot win if we break away from our main aim.'

'It is odd how you can see the truth of that only when you are looking down the barrel of my pistol.' Gonzalez laughed. 'So now you would do anything for me, no?'

'Yes.' Aguilar nodded. 'Anything you ask.'

'Would you kill yourself?' Gonzalez holstered his gun, reached into his jacket, and produced a small pocket pistol, which he unloaded. He replaced a single bullet in the cylinder, closed the gun, then held out the weapon to Sanchez. 'Give it to Aguilar,' he said.

'No!' Sanchez replied. 'If anyone is to be shot then it should be me. I lead the men who broke away from you. Shoot me, Gonzalez, and have done with it.'

'I am not going to shoot anyone

here.' Gonzalez shook his head emphatically. 'Aguilar is going to shoot himself to prove his loyalty.'

He got to his feet, took the smaller gun in his left hand, and drew his pistol again. He walked to where Aguilar was seated and held out the gun containing a single bullet.

'Traitor!' he shouted, putting his mouth close to Aguilar's ear. 'Take the gun. Put it to your head. Pull the trigger and blow out your brains. You are not fit to live with the rest of us.'

Aguilar gazed at the proffered gun and shook his head. 'Please, Gonzalez,' he whined. 'Don't do this. I beg your mercy. Give me another chance and I will prove to you that I can be trusted. I will serve you well.'

'You are a cowardly traitor.' Gonzalez sneered. 'Get down on your knees and I will shoot you if you cannot pull the trigger yourself. I would pardon a traitor if he could see the error of his ways, but I cannot stomach a coward.'

He pressed the muzzle of the small

gun against Aguilar's forehead and squeezed the trigger. Sanchez flinched at the crash of the shot, and stepped back a pace as Aguilar jerked convulsively and fell off the chair with blood spurting from his head. Gonzalez waited until the echoes of the shot had faded before turning to Sanchez.

'He should not have gone after Rosita,' he said. 'I might have spared him but for that. Now it is your turn, Sanchez. How do we settle this problem that exists between us?'

Sanchez shrugged. He knew Gonzalez intimately, and did not expect to leave the cantina without a fight. He was not fast enough with a gun to beat Gonzalez in a straight draw; he knew Gonzalez never fought according to the rules, and realized that he had to bluff his way to safety.

'You want me to come back to you?' he asked.

Gonzalez smiled as he reloaded the small gun. He returned the weapon to his pocket.

'Now you are asking me to trust you, no?' he asked. 'Tell me, would you trust me if I were standing there in your place?' He paused but Sanchez did not answer. 'You see,' he continued, 'it is a difficult problem to solve. I do know that when I start the revolution you will be against me, so perhaps I had better remove you now and save myself a lot of trouble later. But first, tell me why you have come here this morning?'

'I had a message that the guns you were expecting had arrived just across the border and that the Yankees have said they are to be delivered to me. They will give them to me if I use them to stop your revolution.'

Gonzalez half rose from his seat, his mouth gaping in surprise, then he slumped back into the chair. He shook his head, his eyes filled with shock. For a moment he remained motionless, his expression showing disbelief, and then he nodded slowly and exhaled in a long sigh.

'So the Yankees are against another

revolution south of the border, no? They prefer the guns to go to a bandit if he will use them against me. I think I will have to kill you, Sanchez. You have suddenly become too important. Next, you will want to take my place and run my revolution.'

Gonzalez levelled his pistol and aimed at Sanchez, who was shaking his head for he had suddenly thought of a way out for himself.

'Think before you act,' he warned.

'Tell me more.' Gonzalez smiled. 'I'd like to hear what you have in mind that could save your life.'

'If Aguilar told the truth about those two wagons then you have lost them already, and you won't get them back without a big fight. If the message I received about the Yankees wanting to give the guns to me if I oppose you is correct then you don't have to fight for them. All you have to do is pull back and let me go to the Yankees. They will give the guns to me and I will deliver them to you, in return for my life.'

Gonzalez nodded thoughtfully. 'You may not have saved your life entirely but you have postponed your execution. We will go to the river together and see what the situation is, and if I permit you to cross the river to talk to the soldiers you will take some of my men with you as if they belong to you, and they will have orders to kill you should you attempt to double-cross me.'

'I agree to your terms,' Sanchez said without hesitation. 'The sooner we ride the better.'

Gonzalez rose from his seat. He approached Sanchez, and with a quick movement, pulled Sanchez's pistol from its holster.

'Just a precaution,' he said, unloading the weapon before thrusting it back into Sanchez's holster. 'I know you well, Sanchez. You can resist everything but temptation. Now we will ride. I want all those Yankee guns on this side of the border before sundown.'

Sanchez nodded. He was not happy with the situation, but he had put a stay on his execution and that gave him time in which to think of a way he might thwart Gonzalez, although he was keenly aware that time was running out.

8

Moran lay in the undergrowth on the American bank of the Rio Grande and watched the wagon stranded in midstream. The sun was almost overhead, glittering on the surface of the river, and the heat was terrific. He felt that it had been a long morning. He was holding his rifle. His pale eyes were narrowed against the midday glare as he looked for movement across the river. He could see men moving around over there but they were careful not to present themselves as targets, for Lieutenant Anderson and his alert soldiers would open fire if they paused long enough to be shot at.

The stranded wagon occupied Moran's attention, and he was wondering how he could recover it from the river. They had already made one attempt to hitch fresh horses to it and pull it back to American soil, but the Mexicans opposing them were too many and the attempt ended in failure. They suffered casualties — two soldiers dead and three wounded. Now all Moran could do was guard against any attempt by Gonzalez to snatch the stranded supplies and escape with them.

Lieutenant Anderson came slithering through the undergrowth to crawl up beside Moran. He was breathless, his face red, beaded with sweat.

'There's activity lower down the stream, Captain,' Anderson reported. 'About a dozen Mexicans are crossing over to our side. It looks like they're going to try and outflank us.'

'I've been expecting something like that,' Moran replied. 'Deal with it, Lieutenant. I'll watch the wagon. I expect Gonzalez will make a try for the supplies while we are distracted by his diversion. Leave a couple of men to back me in case they attempt another direct assault.'

'Yes, sir, will do.' Anderson turned and crawled away.

Moran heard the lieutenant giving

orders to his men, and the brush crackled as most of them moved away to guard against a flank attack. Moran continued to watch his front. He checked his weapons and ammunition, then tried to relax. In the back of his mind was the hope that reinforcements were coming, but he could not rely on that. He saw a Mexican on the far bank jump up from cover and run a dozen yards to his right, as if attempting to draw fire. The man disappeared into the brush, but a moment later he reappeared and ran back to his original position.

Moran did not move. He could only wait, and resist any serious effort by the Mexicans to recover the wagon. He watched closely for signs of Gonzalez, but did not see the white horse which the bandit rode. He sensed that Gonzalez had gone to fetch more men. Time seemed to drag, but he controlled his impatience. This was a waiting game and he would play his part to the full.

He stiffened into full alertness when shooting broke out to his left. He looked around but saw nothing. Anderson's men were in action and a fierce fire-fight raged for many minutes. Moran kept watching the far bank of the river, expecting some activity there now Gonzalez had his diversion going. When he saw a dozen mounted figures appear and enter the river, followed by two riders, each leading a spare horse, he checked his rifle. The Mexicans splashed through the water towards the wagon and spray sparkled in the sunlight.

Moran jacked a shell into the breech of the Springfield and looked through the sights. He waited until the riders were within good range and drew a bead on the foremost Mexican. When he fired, the man pitched out of his saddle, disappeared momentarily into the river, and then his head became visible and he was borne away by the current. The remaining riders reined in, disconcerted by the disappearance of their leader. Moran took advantage of the situation and sent a stream of lead into them, hitting two more men. The survivors turned their horses and went hurrying back to the opposite bank.

The Mexicans leading the spare horses turned them loose and concentrated on getting clear. Moran hurried them on their way with accurate shooting, and another Mexican vacated his saddle before the survivors reached the bank and found cover. Moran turned his head to the left and listened to the shooting on the flank, which was dying away to desultory shots. He was satisfied that the attempt to get to the wagon had been stopped. He reloaded his rifle and wiped sweat from his face. It was going to be a long, hard afternoon.

Lieutenant Anderson returned to Moran's side.

'About twelve Mexicans tried to rush us, Captain,' he reported. 'We shot the hell out of them.'

'Good work,' Moran commended. 'There was an attempt to bring fresh harness horses to the wagon. But there's no way that trick is going to work. Let's hope we'll have some reinforcements here before sundown.

'Sergeant Johnson is on the main trail to Del Rio, and he'll direct any reinforcements to this spot,' Anderson said confidently. 'I'll bring my men back to cover the wagon out there. I'm thinking Gonzalez will try a frontal attack next.'

'All we have to do is stop them,' Moran observed. 'But there is another chance. I sent a Mexican across the river earlier to contact Pedro Sanchez, and if Sanchez turns up with his men then Gonzalez will have to think again about getting his hands on the supplies.'

'In my experience you can't trust any Mexican, sir.' Anderson looked doubtful, and Moran smiled.

'I've been ordered to hand over the supplies to Sanchez, who is against Gonzalez, so I don't have any choice in the matter, and I expect Sanchez will take a hand with us now the chips are down.'

Moran settled to watch and wait. Anderson returned to his men and positioned them along the river-bank. When he came back to Moran he was frowning.

'A Mexican couple have ridden into our rearguard, Captain,' he reported. 'One of them is a girl and she says you know her — says her name is Rosita Gonzalez.'

'I do know her!' Moran frowned. 'What the devil is she doing back here?'

'She wants to talk to you,' Anderson said.

'Take over here while I talk to her,' Moran eased back from the river-bank, stood up, and walked to the rear carrying his Springfield. He saw Rosita and Gomez standing with two of the cavalrymen who were acting as rearguard.

'I didn't expect to see you again,' Moran commented. 'I assumed you would be at your aunt's ranch by now.'

'I thought I would be safe there,' Rosita explained the events that had taken place. 'We were heading back across the border when we found Aguilar lying wounded on the trail this side of the river. I think he was heading back to my aunt's ranch to try and capture me again.'

'I sent him to find Pedro Sanchez.' Moran frowned. 'He had some great news for Sanchez, and when I last saw Aguilar he was eager to get back across the river to locate his boss. Something must have happened to change his plans.'

'There is a village just across the river where he could have found someone to take a message to Sanchez,' Rosita observed.

'I'd like to go there and find out for myself,' Moran observed, 'but I'm not permitted to cross the river while on duty.'

'I could go there for you,' Rosita volunteered.

'And why would you do that?' Moran studied her expressionless face. 'You must have heard the shooting as you

191

came up. We are fighting your father's men.'

'I know.' She nodded. 'We saw one of your wagons heading under escort to Del Rio, and the other is stranded in the middle of the river. My father can bring up a hundred men if he needs them, so you cannot win this fight, Captain, unless you have help, and I am ready to help you for I am totally against my father.'

'We'll have reinforcements here before long.' Moran sounded confident although his face was harsh. 'I don't wish to involve you in this business, Señorita Gonzalez, and your father would not be too pleased with you for helping his enemies. He is determined to get the supplies at any cost.'

'He is not pleased with me.' Rosita said sadly. 'He held me prisoner at home because he wanted me to marry someone of his choice.' She glanced at the attentive Gomez. 'He even imprisoned Alfredo and threatened to kill him because I love him.'

'I will find Pedro Sanchez for you, Captain,' Gomez said. 'I will do anything that will help stop Rosita's father.'

'Thanks for the offer, but I cannot use you,' Moran said. 'I suggest you both get away from here and find somewhere that is safe until this business has been settled.'

'We'll go back into Mexico and try to find Sanchez,' Rosita said firmly. 'My father must be stopped.'

'I have the feeling that death is the only thing that will stop him,' Moran mused, shaking his head. 'I'm hoping it does not come to that, but I don't see him pulling out while the supplies are here. Now if you will excuse me, I must get back to duty.'

He turned abruptly and hurried back to the river-bank, glancing over his shoulder once to see that Rosita and Gomez had mounted their horses and were preparing to ride out. He dismissed them from his mind and looked at the wagon stranded in midstream. There were no Mexicans in sight and a heavy silence lay over the area. He dropped into cover beside Lieutenant Anderson.

'Nothing to report, Captain,' Anderson said. 'It's quiet over there.'

'Too quiet,' Moran observed.

'I could take some men and a couple of spare horses out to the wagon under covering fire and attempt to bring it back to this side,' Anderson said hopefully.

'I've considered that, and I think the wagon is safer where it is.' Moran shook his head. 'We'd lose too many men trying that. We'll watch for now and hope our reinforcements will show up before Gonzalez decides to make another move.'

They remained motionless but watchful, and time passed slowly. The ripple of the water against the bank was strangely soothing, but the glare of the bright sunlight was giving Moran a headache. He pressed the thumb and two fingers of his left hand against his eyes and relished the easement afforded by the action, but when he opened his eyes again he saw figures on the opposite bank. He checked his ammunition and picked up his rifle.

A line of riders appeared from cover across the river. They were all holding rifles. A white horse was prominent among them, and Moran picked up his field glasses and focused on its rider. A thrill passed through him when he recognized Gonzalez, and he exhaled in a long sigh as he waited.

'It looks like they are going to attack,' Lieutenant Anderson observed. 'I count twenty of them, and I don't think there are enough of them to succeed.'

'They'll advance under covering fire,' Moran replied. 'Tell your men to hold their fire until I start shooting.'

Anderson nodded and withdrew. Moran could hear him calling orders to the troopers. The Mexicans were waiting for orders from Gonzalez, who sat his horse as if he were a statue, gazing at the stranded wagon. There was complete silence around the river.

Then Gonzalez waved a hand and set spurs to his horse. He splashed into the river and sent his mount forward in great leaps, raking the animal's flanks unmercifully with his vicious spurs. The line of Mexicans followed behind him, two of whom were leading harness horses in anticipation of hauling the wagon ashore.

Moran waited until Gonzalez was halfway between the opposite bank and the wagon before raising his rifle into the aim. He drew a bead on the Mexican leader and squeezed the trigger when the foresight was centred on Gonzalez's chest. He hardly felt the recoil of the Springfield as he watched Gonzalez intently. The big Mexican was riding flamboyantly, holding his reins in his left hand and waving his rifle in his right hand. His mouth was agape, and Moran could hear him shouting defiance. The white horse seemed to stumble as Moran's bullet struck Gonzalez, and the Mexican was slammed backwards in his saddle by the impact of the bullet. His arms flew wide. He dropped his rifle into the river and made a superhuman effort to remain in leather but lost his balance and pitched sideways into the water.

The white horse whirled immediately and set off back to the far bank, splashing mightily as it sought to get clear of the following Mexicans. The disappearance of Gonzalez set the rest of his men into action, and they began shooting wildly as they forced their horses towards the motionless wagon. At that moment the troopers opened fire and poured a stream of hot lead at the advancing line of men. Bullets whipped around the Mexicans, throwing up spurts of water. A horse went down, and then another.

Moran watched for Gonzalez to surface, and shortly saw the man's head appear. Gonzalez seemed to be unconscious — he was not trying to swim — and drifted with the pull of the current. One of his men turned aside from the wagon and made a desperate effort to reach him but Gonzalez was carried around a bend and Moran lost sight of him. Moran turned his attention to the Mexicans still attempting to reach the wagon and fired rapidly. He could see bullets kicking up spurts of water around the Mexicans, and they soon decided against pressing their attack. They turned and went streaming back to their own side of the river.

An uneasy silence returned as the surviving riders found cover on the far bank and disappeared from sight. Moran lowered his rifle and looked around. He had a feeling that the Mexicans would consider a frontal attack as being too expensive and would not attempt another. They had lost nearly half their force and their leader had been carried away by the current. Moran reloaded his Springfield and waited . . .

$\star$ $\star$ $\star$

Gonzalez had cursed when he and Sanchez reached the river from the village. He reined into cover and gazed across the water at the stranded wagon. Sanchez dismounted to rest his horse and dropped to his knees behind a tree. He could see Yankee soldiers on the far bank, and his pulses quickened at the thought that the message he had received about the shipment of weapons was true. He watched Gonzalez intently without appearing to do so. Gonzalez stood behind a tree and called for Ramos, whom he had left in command of the wagons.

'What happened, Ramos?' he demanded angrily. 'All you had to do was bring the wagons across the river. I thought a child could do that with no trouble so I left you in charge, and now I have returned what do I find? One wagon is missing; the other is stuck in the middle of the river with both horses dead, and there are Yankee soldiers on the far bank. What do you think they are going to do when I send you out there to bring in that wagon?'

'It was not my fault, Gonzalez,' Ramos blustered. 'One wagon broke a wheel on the other side of the river and

I left it under guard while it was being repaired. I did not know there were Yankee soldiers coming. I was halfway across the river with that wagon out there when the soldiers shot the horses. There was no way I could move the wagon.'

'Have you tried to get to the wagon?' Gonzalez demanded.

'Yes, but the soldiers beat us back. I sent a party across the river lower down to cut off the soldiers but they chased them off. While they were over there, Rodriguez went on alone to look for the second wagon and found it gone. The soldiers had changed the wheel and driven it away. He followed its tracks and decided that the wagon is heading to Del Rio with a small escort of soldiers.'

'I've told you how to get those wagons without a fight,' Sanchez said.

Gonzalez sneered. 'Do you think I would listen to anything you suggested?' he demanded. 'Ramos, take ten men and cross the river higher up.

Catch up with the wagon going to Del Rio and recapture it. Bring it back across the border safely and you might live to see tomorrow.'

Ramos nodded and turned away quickly, relieved at having got off so lightly. Gonzalez crouched beside Sanchez until Ramos had departed.

'There's no one I can trust,' Gonzalez mused bitterly. 'I have to do everything myself. Rodriguez, I have a job for you.' He waited until a tall, thin Mexican came to stand before him. 'I want you to watch Sanchez and keep him here while I take some men out to the wagon in the river and bring it in. Tell the men to get ready. We'll have to take two spare horses with us to hitch to the wagon. The rest of the men will cover us from here. Have you got that?'

Rodriguez nodded and drew his pistol. 'Come with me, Sanchez,' he ordered.

Gonzalez waited until his men had grouped together for the attack before going to his horse. He swung into the saddle, checked his weapons, and then rode to the river-bank. His men gathered around him, and he checked that two spare horses were included in the party. He studied the wagon for some moments and then shifted his gaze to the far bank. He saw no sign of Yankee soldiers and gave the signal for his men to advance. They rode into the river and pressed forward.

Water splashed around them as the horses pranced through the belly-high river. Gonzalez pushed into the lead, and was halfway to the stranded wagon when he saw movement on the far bank as Moran lifted his Springfield into the aim and fired. At that moment Gonzalez's horse put its right foreleg into a hole in the river bed and jerked to the left to maintain its balance. Gonzalez yelled in shock when Moran's bullet struck him high in the left shoulder, and sawed on his reins, almost pulling his horse down. The animal jumped and Gonzalez pitched out of the saddle. He dropped his rifle as he plunged into the river. Shooting erupted as he filled his lungs with air just before his head submerged, and he swam to the right before breaking the surface. He played dead and let the current carry him away from the crossing, but he watched the far shore and saw soldiers firing rapidly at his men. He waited until he had passed around a bend in the river before forcing himself to his feet and wading to the Mexican bank, where he dragged himself ashore and dropped limply in the dust. Two of his men were riding along the bank towards him from the crossing; one of them was leading the white horse.

Gonzalez grunted as he pushed himself into a sitting position. He checked his left shoulder and found a flesh wound above the collar bone. The bullet had bored through the flesh without striking the bone and the wound was hardly bleeding. He got to his feet when his men arrived, swung into his saddle, and rode into cover before heading back to the crossing. He heard no further shooting as he rode, and dismissed the idea of trying to take the stranded wagon by a frontal attack.

'We lost seven men in that attack,' Rodriguez reported when Gonzalez reached him.

Gonzalez confronted Sanchez, who was sitting quietly behind some bushes.

'It is time for you to go to the Yankee soldiers and tell them who you are,' Gonzalez said. 'You will be accompanied by Rodriguez, who will shoot you if you try to fool me. You will collect that wagon in the river and bring it out here, and then we will decide what to do. In the meantime, Ramos should be heading back with the wagon that is on the way to Del Rio. While you are talking to the Yankees, I will visit Doctor Lopez in the village. For your own sake, Sanchez, do not try to get smart. It would pain me to have to kill you at this time.'

'You'd better pull all your men back to the village,' Sanchez suggested. 'The Yankee soldiers will not hand over the wagon if you are still here in force. I will cross higher up and approach them from a different direction.'

Gonzalez nodded. 'Rodriguez, you will go with Sanchez, and kill him if he tries to warn the Yankees of this plan.'

Sanchez made no comment and went for his horse, accompanied by Rodriguez, and they rode off to cross the river lower down the stream. Gonzalez summoned the rest of his men and led them to the village.

9

Ramos rode at the head of ten men, determined to take the wagon heading for Del Rio. They crossed the river upstream from the spot where the second wagon was stranded, reached the main trail leading to the distant town, and turned left. Fresh wagon tracks showed plainly in the dust and Ramos spurred his horse and set off at a gallop in pursuit. An hour later they topped a rise and saw the wagon a mile ahead, with thin streamers of dust rising from its churning wheels. Two soldiers were on the driving seat of the wagon — their horses tied behind — and three troopers were riding escort.

'Luis, go with four men and circle to get ahead of the wagon. I will give you time to get into position before I move in from this direction. The soldiers will put up a fight, so we must kill them quickly.'

Luis rode off to the right, seeking cover as he and his followers circled to an ambush position. Ramos remained in cover behind the rise until the wagon passed over a crest ahead, and then led the remainder of his men along the trail to close up on the wagon. The trail wound like a serpent through the rugged wilderness. Brush grew in profusion, affording plenty of cover. Ramos moved in, and after a calculated interval he pushed his horse into a gallop and chased after the wagon.

Sergeant Johnson heard the pounding of hoofs at his back and twisted in his saddle, He clawed his pistol out of its holster when he saw Mexicans bearing down on him from the rear and shouted a warning to his men. At that instant shooting broke out from ahead of the wagon and Johnson jerked around to see half a dozen Mexicans emerging from cover to block the trail. They came forward, shooting rapidly.

The driver of the wagon dropped the reins, pitched off his seat, and the wagon slewed across the trail as the horses halted.

The Mexicans fired rapidly at the soldiers, who immediately returned fire. Sergeant Johnson, a veteran with twenty years' service to his credit, triggered his Army Colt. He saw his first target pitch out of leather, but as he drew a bead on a second Mexican a bullet from ahead of the wagon slammed between his shoulder blades, bored into his heart; and it was as if the whole world exploded inside him. Blood spurted out through the exit wound just under his sternum and he was dead before he fell from his saddle. The rest of the escort quickly suffered the same fate, and all were down in the dust before the Mexicans closed in around the wagon. One soldier, moving feebly, was shot in the head.

Ramos was jubilant. He had lost three men to the soldiers but manpower was not a problem south of the border.

'José, get up in that driving seat and we'll head back across the river,' he ordered.

One of the Mexicans tied his horse behind the wagon and scuttled on to the driving seat. He snatched up the reins and swung the team around, cracked the whip, and sent the two animals back along the trail. Ramos took the lead, turned off the trail, and headed for the river.

* * *

Captain Manning had pushed along relentlessly from Del Rio with his four tough Texas Rangers behind him. They had travelled many miles since dawn and Manning, knowing the area intimately, was wondering what had happened to Captain Moran since leaving him in the gully the day before. When he heard the popping sound of distant shots ahead he immediately spurred his horse and sent it forward at its best pace. He hammered over a crest and saw several uniformed figures sprawled on the trail. Two horses were standing nearby with lowered heads, their reins trailing on the ground. A banner of dust far ahead marked the progress of a wagon leaving the grim scene, and Manning narrowed his eyes when he recognized Mexicans.

'Let's get those murdering greasers before they can cross the river,' Manning shouted. 'We must keep that wagon on our side of the border. Start earning your pay, men. We've got those Mexes right where we want them.'

The Rangers drew their pistols and pushed their horses into a gallop. Dust flew as they chased after the wagon, and brassy sunlight glinted on their levelled weapons.

Pedro Sanchez, accompanied by Rodriguez, forded the river above the spot where the wagon was stranded and made a detour to approach the position of the soldiers from the north. A rear guard arose from cover and challenged them. Sanchez reined in.

'Your officer wishes to see me,' he said. 'I received a message from him this morning. I am Pedro Sanchez.'

'Never heard of you,' the guard replied. 'But follow me and I'll take you to the captain.'

He led the way to the river, and Moran arose from his position to confront them.

Sanchez spoke quickly. 'I am Pedro Sanchez. I received a message this morning that you wished to talk to me.'

'Who delivered the message?' Moran demanded.

'A man named Tomas Aguilar. He rides with me.'

'Where is Aguilar?' Moran glanced around. 'Hasn't he come back with you? I need him to identify you, Sanchez.'

'He was wounded, and is in the village just across the river. Gonzalez and his men are withdrawing to the village. Gonzalez was hurt when he went into the river, but the wound is not serious.'

'He has a charmed life,' Moran observed. 'I have been ordered to hand over two wagonloads of supplies and weapons to you, if you are Pedro Sanchez. Can you prevent the wagons falling into Gonzalez's hands when you get them into Mexico?'

'I have many men coming here, and we shall await their arrival.'

Lieutenant Anderson approached, and Sanchez, smiling in relief, called a greeting to him.

'I know that officer,' Sanchez said to Moran, 'and he can vouch for me. I sold some horses to the army last year, and that officer handled the deal.'

'Can you verify this man's identity, Lieutenant?' Moran asked.

'Yes, Captain. Pedro Sanchez is a well known horse thief hereabouts.'

'You'd better send a galloper after the other wagon and have it brought back,' Moran ordered. 'The sooner we get this business settled the better.'

Anderson nodded and went back to his men. A few moments later, one of the troopers rode out at a gallop, heading for the trail to Del Rio. Moran studied Sanchez, and did not like what he saw. From what he knew of Mexicans, he would not trust any of them, but he was under orders.

'We can do nothing now but wait,' Moran said. 'Tell me about Gonzalez, Sanchez. You used to ride with him, didn't you?'

'Until he got the big idea about having a revolution,' Sanchez replied. 'It was then I broke away from him because I could see it was a situation nobody could win, especially we poor bandits. And if Gonzalez thinks he can start a civil war with what you have brought in two wagons then he is a bigger fool than I took him for.'

'Hadn't we better go back across the river and wait for the rest of our men to show up?' Rodriguez cut in. 'We should keep an eye on Gonzalez. He is one tricky *hombre*.'

'With your permission, Captain, we will do as Rodriguez suggests,' Sanchez said instantly. 'I'll come back when my men arrive. There will be no trouble with Gonzalez when we get the two

213

wagons into Mexico.'

Moran nodded. 'That's OK by me. Leave someone on your side of the river to signal me if Gonzalez returns there from the village.'

Rodriguez turned away immediately, but Sanchez paused and looked meaningfully at Moran, who frowned. Sanchez pointed at Rodriguez with his left hand while tapping the butt of his holstered pistol. Moran shook his head, not understanding the sign language. Rodriguez turned when he realized that Sanchez had not immediately followed him, saw the signal Sanchez was trying to convey, and cursed loudly as he made a play for his holstered pistol. Moran's right hand was down by his side, and when he saw Rodriguez's quick movement he set his own hand into motion.

Moran palmed his Colt with practised ease. Rodriguez cleared leather and lifted his weapon, aiming at Sanchez instead of Moran, who waited a fraction of a second to catch Rodriguez's intention. As Rodriguez cocked his pistol, Moran triggered his gun, aiming for Rodriguez's chest. The crash of their shots blended almost as one and echoes flew. Rodriguez jerked under the strike of Moran's bullet, tried desperately to bring his gun to bear on Moran, but lost his grip on the weapon as his life ended precipitately. He fell to the ground, kicking spasmodically, his feet disturbing the dust, and blood spurting from the centre of his chest. Sanchez went down at the same moment, as if they had been joined together by a single rope, and a spreading patch of blood appeared on his right thigh, caused by Rodriguez's bullet.

Moran holstered his gun and bent over Sanchez. Blood was running swiftly from the bullet wound in the Mexican's upper leg. Moran pressed a thumb against the wound to stop the bleeding. Lieutenant Anderson came running to Moran's side.

'What happened, Captain?' Anderson demanded.

Moran shook his head. 'I'm about to ask Sanchez the same question,' he replied, and looked at Sanchez.

Sanchez looked up at Moran. His face was pale beneath its colour and his dark eyes were filled with pain. He spoke through clenched teeth.

'Rodriguez is Gonzalez's man,' he said. 'Gonzalez told him to shoot me if I tried to tell you the truth.'

'Which is?' Moran demanded.

Sanchez explained in a pain-laden tone. Moran nodded and moved back. He glanced at Lieutenant Anderson.

'Do what you can for him, Lieutenant,' he ordered. 'I'll watch the river.'

*   *   *

Ramos and the Mexicans taking the supply wagon to the river were highly delighted with their prize, but their glee vanished when someone heard the sound of rapidly approaching hoofs from their rear and called a warning. Ramos glanced over his shoulder, saw a group of riders chasing after them, and drew his pistol.

'Keep going for the river,' he yelled to the wagon driver. 'Get across, whatever you do. The rest of you drop back. We've got some more work to do.'

The wagon continued, grinding through the short brush leading to the water's edge. The rest of the men reined in, turned their horses, and drew their weapons.

'Spread out!' Ramos cried. 'Let them get close, and then make sure of them.'

The Mexicans deployed. Some of them dismounted and dropped into cover. The five Texas Rangers came on swiftly, and their guns began to blast almost before they drew within range. Captain Manning held his knotted reins between his teeth, holding two pistols in his hands. He saw Ramos standing tall in the brush and snapped a shot at the Mexican without appearing to aim. Ramos jerked, twisted, then fell to the ground. The next instant rapid gunfire battered the silence and echoes fled. Two Mexicans fell instantly, and one of the Rangers slumped over the neck of his horse before pitching sideways to the ground.

The fallen Ranger's horse galloped up beside Captain Manning, and he glanced around quickly, saw the fallen rider, and returned his attention to the Mexicans. He fired his big pistols alternately, shooting at the fleeting figures that arose to resist him. He reached their ragged line, and blinked when one of them fired a pistol almost in his face, the slug tearing through the brim of his Stetson. He replied in kind, and saw the Mexican jerk before twisting away. He rode towards the river, intent on stopping the wagon.

The wagon driver heard the pounding hoofs approaching from his rear and glanced over his shoulder. He was whipping the two horses desperately, aware that he had to cross the river to be safe. When he saw the big figure of Manning coming up fast he drew his pistol and half turned to face his rear, cocking his gun and lifting it to draw a bead on his attacker. Manning fired his right-hand gun and smoke blossomed from the muzzle. The driver felt the smack of hot lead in his left shoulder and dropped his pistol in shock. He fell off the driving seat and sprawled across the hind quarters of the two horses before sliding sideways to the ground, and he screamed hoarsely as a churning wagon wheel crunched over his head.

Manning spurred his horse. He holstered his guns as he drew level with the running team and leaned sideways to grab the reins of the nearer horse. When he hauled on the reins the two animals stopped surprisingly quickly and stood trembling. Manning looked ahead. He could see the river barely one hundred yards ahead. The shooting had tailed off, and he looked over his shoulder but could not see any of the Mexicans still standing. He stayed by the wagon, reloading his guns, and, one by one, three of his Rangers converged on him.

'Where's Bennett?' Manning demanded.
'He's dead, Captain,' Wade replied.

Manning grimaced and shook his head.

'Put him on the wagon,' he said. We'll have to bury him later. Wade, tie your horse behind the wagon and get up on that seat. We'll head for the river and the soldiers, and don't stop for anything. I guess Captain Moran must be wondering where in hell these supplies have gotten to.'

They headed back to the trail, continued south, and had travelled barely three miles when a trooper appeared ahead, coming towards them from the river and riding as if chased by the Devil. Manning called a halt and they waited for the cavalryman to arrive. The soldier explained the situation at the river crossing. Manning wasted no time.

'One of you stay with the wagon and defend it if attacked,' he ordered. 'Let the soldier boy drive it now. You other two follow me. We'll split the breeze and see what we can do at the river.'

Manning and two of the Rangers rode on ahead. The silence seemed to throb in their ears after the fight with the Mexicans. When they neared the main crossing at the river two cavalrymen jumped up out of cover to challenge them, and Manning dismounted. One of the soldiers led him to Moran's position. Manning looked around critically as Moran came to him, and his eyes glinted when he saw the stranded wagon standing up to its axles in the river.

'How you doing, Captain?' Manning asked. 'We just stopped a bunch of Mexicans running off with that wagon you started back to Del Rio. It's on its way back here now.'

'I'm hoping for military reinforcements before long,' Moran said. 'And when they arrive I'll get that wagon out of the river. I've seen Pedro Sanchez. He's gone back across the river to the village. The trouble is, Gonzalez is over there, too, and there's no telling what tricks he'll pull to grab the supplies.'

'If I can get Gonzalez over to this side of the river I'll arrest him,'

Manning said. 'There's a price on his head over here.'

'He's too tricky to fall for anything we might try.' Moran shook his head. 'With any luck he'll try something against Sanchez and get himself killed.'

'I could take off my badge and ride into Mexico,' Manning mused. 'I've been across there several times, and I might be able to do something about Gonzalez.'

'I wouldn't bet on it.' Moran shook his head. 'And I'd like nothing better than to go with you and put a kink in Gonzalez's tail.'

'You're not in uniform so there's no reason why you shouldn't cross the line.' Manning grinned.

'My duty is plain.' Moran shook his head. 'I've got to hand the supplies over to Sanchez, and when I've done that my job is over. Gonzalez is not my concern.'

'It's a different matter for me.' Manning nodded. 'Gonzalez has been a thorn in my side for years, and if I could nail him then a lot of people this side of the border will be able to sleep peacefully in their beds at night. You seem to have matters in hand around here, so me and my men just might take a look around on the other side of the river.'

'Don't stir up trouble until my job is done,' Moran said.

The big Texas Ranger nodded emphatically. His expression changed suddenly and he reached into his breast pocket.

'I almost forgot,' he said. 'I picked up a wire addressed to you before I left Del Rio.'

He handed the wire to Moran who opened it quickly and scanned the message.

'Is something wrong?' Manning demanded, noting Moran's change of expression.

'A slight change of orders,' Moran replied thoughtfully. 'I must destroy both wagons and the supplies if they look like falling into Gonzalez's hands . . .'

★ ★ ★

After leaving Moran, Rosita and Gomez crossed the river into Mexico and headed towards the village. When they reached the outskirts of the community, Gomez called a halt.

'I want you to stay here, Rosita, while I ride in and look around,' he said.

'You're not going anywhere without me,' she responded quickly. 'If my father is here he will shoot you on sight. It would be better if I rode in alone. I can always say I am looking for my father, and none of his men would harm me.'

Gomez shook his head. 'It took me a long time to find you and spring you loose from your father's influence,' he said, 'and I'm not taking any chances now. We both know what Gonzalez is like. I wouldn't trust him as far as I could throw his horse.'

'He wouldn't kill me — that's for sure,' Rosita said firmly. 'But he'd shoot you without hesitation. Please be sensible and let me go and look around. I don't have to show myself. I'll just find out who is in the village and what they are doing. It would be simple for me.'

Gomez shook his head. 'We'll do this my way. Don't argue with me. Stay here with the horses and I'll be back in a few minutes.'

'If you kill my father I'll never speak to you again,' Rosita said emphatically.

'I won't pull my gun on him unless he draws first.'

Rosita heaved a sigh and dismounted. Gomez slid out of his saddle and handed her the reins of his mount. He drew his pistol from its holster, checked its load, and then eased it back into leather.

'Remember, you stay here,' he cautioned.

When she did not reply he turned and walked along the street towards the cantina. Rosita watched him for a moment, and then led the horses behind the adobe stable to hitch them to a rail of the corral out back. She returned to watching the street but did not disobey Gomez, who was walking quickly towards the cantina. His dark eyes were alert, his right hand down at his side, close to the butt of his pistol. The village seemed deserted, but it was siesta time and the heat of the day was packed into every corner of the dusty street. The breeze that came from the west held the intensity of a furnace. The silence was heavy, oppressive, and contained a hint of hostility.

A Mexican appeared in the doorway of the cantina and paused to look casually around the street. When he saw Gomez he started, stared intently, and then dropped his hand to his holstered gun. Gomez waited, and, when the man began to draw his pistol, he set his own right hand into motion. He grasped the butt of his weapon, cocked it as it cleared leather, and squeezed the trigger when his foresight covered the man's chest. He was more than a second faster, and the pistol bucked in his hand as it spurted smoke. The crash of the shot echoed around the town. The man jerked backwards in the doorway when the bullet smacked into his chest. He fell awkwardly, and only his upturned boots showed in the doorway when he finally stilled in death.

Gomez turned and dived into the alley beside the cantina. Several dogs were barking at the gunshot. He ran halfway along the alley to pause at a window which gave him a view of the interior of the building. When he peered inside he saw Sanchez standing at the bar with Martinez. There was no sign of Gonzalez, but he recognized some of the dozen men also present as mostly Gonzalez riders, and some of them were in the process of hurrying out the door in response to the shot, stepping carelessly over the fallen figure in the doorway.

He went on to the far end of the alley, paused to peer around the deserted back lots, and hurriedly stepped out of the alley and flattened himself against the rear wall of the cantina. He could still hear the fading echoes of his shot growling away into the far distance. His thoughts were fleeting. Where was Gonzalez? He wanted to shoot Rosita's father for the way he had been treated, despite his assurance to Rosita that he would not shoot first. But he was aware that he and Rosita would never be free to marry while Gonzalez lived.

Voices sounded in the alley. Gomez risked a look and saw two men coming along it from the street. He moved quickly, hurried to the rear door of the cantina, and slipped inside the back room. Maria, the wife of Martinez, was preparing vegetables for a meal. She looked around quickly at Gomez's entrance, noted the drawn gun in his hand, and went on with her chore without evincing shock or surprise at his unexpected appearance.

'Can you tell me if Gonzalez is in the village?' Gomez demanded.

'He was shot at the river and is with the medico,' Maria replied, 'I hope he dies; him and his revolution.'

'I hope so, too,' Gomez said. 'If he dies it will save me the trouble of shooting him.'

'Shooting is too good for the likes of him. Honest people go in fear of their lives when he is around. Gonzalez is not even an honest bandit. He robs poor peons and steals from his own kind. If you shoot him you will be doing all of us a great favour. But he is not easy to kill.'

'He would make a great president if I don't shoot him,' Gomez observed. 'He has all the vices needed to run the country.'

Maria laughed. Gomez turned to the door and peered out at the back lots. He saw no sign of the two men who had been in the alley, and departed to skirt the rear of the buildings fronting the street until he reached the outer edge of the village. He walked along the outer side of the last house, making for the front corner on the street, and paused to peer around it. He knew the village well, and picked out the medico's house on the opposite side of the street. His gaze roved on. Three men were standing in the doorway of the cantina, talking loudly; the body of the dead man had been dragged out of the doorway.

A door banged echoingly and Gomez looked around to see that two men had emerged from the medico's house. He recognized Gonzalez and had started to leave his cover when he heard a shout from along the street. He paused, shifted his gaze, and shock filled him when he saw Rosita coming at a run towards her father. He stepped back into cover, stifling a groan, and watched as the girl he loved hurried forward. He lifted his gun and aimed at Gonzalez, but changed his mind and lowered the weapon.

'Rosita,' he yelled. 'Go back! Get out of here.'

Gonzalez, his left shoulder heavily bandaged, swung around, saw Gomez, and uttered an angry bellow. He drew his pistol and fired three quick shots at Gomez, who ducked back behind the corner as soon as he saw the hostile movement. Bullets thudded into the adobe corner where he was standing and dust flew. Gomez thrust his gun hand around the corner and fired a warning shot over Gonzalez's head. When he looked out along the street he saw Gonzalez running for the cover of the cantina, dragging Rosita with him. Gomez hurried him on his way with a slug that kicked up dust beside Gonzalez's right boot heel.

The man who had emerged from the medico's house with Gonzalez was still standing in the doorway, his gun in its holster, apparently shocked by the sudden action. Gomez covered him, but out of the corner of his eye he saw two of the three men in front of the cantina begin moving towards him, drawing their pistols. Gomez opened fire on them and they dived for cover, returning fire. The man in front of the medico's house finally got into the action, and his bullets smacked into the corner as Gomez hurled himself back around it.

Gomez dropped to one knee and peered around the corner. Two of

Gonzalez's men were on the move again, running towards his corner, and he paused to reload before engaging them. His first shot hit the foremost of the pair. The man went down as if his legs had been kicked from under him, and the following man blundered over the fallen body and fell to his knees. Gomez shot him in the chest.

The man who had been with Gonzalez in the medico's house was nowhere in sight. Gomez grimaced and looked around. There was nowhere he could hide, and he realized that he needed to get back to his horse. He ran across the street and headed for the opposite back lots, intent on collecting his horse and moving out. He could not fight the number of men at Gonzalez's disposal in the village, and there was no way he could rescue Rosita from her father's hands.

He hurried along the back lots toward the stable, his alert mind thrusting up a course of action which he knew was unrealistic, for he had to run now and fight later, when the odds would be more in his favour. He was passing the back of the medico's house when a man stepped out of the alley beside it and started shooting at him. Gomez dived to the ground as the first of three bullets crackled in his right ear. The second bullet struck his right arm just above the elbow, and the shock of it sent his gun spinning from his grasp. The third shot missed him, and he hurled himself sideways in a desperate attempt to pick up his pistol.

'Touch the gun and you are dead!' his attacker called in a hoarse tone.

Gomez looked around, saw a steady gun muzzle pointing at his heart, and slowly raised his hands.

'On your feet and make for the cantina,' the Mexican said. 'Gonzalez has been telling us what he will do to you when you are caught, and I can't wait to see it happen.'

Gomez got to his feet, walked through the alley, and crossed the street to the door of the cantina. It was gloomy inside and he paused on the threshold to get his bearings. Sanchez was at the bar, conversing with Martinez. Gonzalez was at the back of the large room, seated at a table with Rosita by his side, and the grin that came to his face when he saw Gomez with his hands raised warned Gomez that he would find no mercy here.

10

When Sanchez left Moran to ride back to the village across the river he realized that if he did not kill Gonzalez then he would die. He reloaded his pistol as he reached the river, and halted his horse for a moment to look at the wagon stranded in the water. There were no signs of Mexicans on the far bank, but he knew they were around, and none were his men. Gonzalez would be taking no chances. When he rode on, Sanchez tried to work out how best to use the situation for his own survival.

When he reached the far bank several Mexicans arose to cover him with their guns, their hard expressions warning him that they had received definite orders from Gonzalez.

'What did the *gringo* captain say?' Emilio demanded.

'He will hand over the wagons when

all Gonzalez's men have left the village,' Sanchez said.

Emilio laughed. 'If you tell Gonzalez that he will shoot you in the head.'

'It is the truth, whatever you may think. A party of soldiers will come across the river to check.'

'They cannot cross the river in uniform.' Emilio shrugged. 'You will have to do better than that if you hope to see the sun go down today.'

'I am only telling you what the *gringo* told me.' Sanchez scowled. 'You'd better start pulling the rest of your men back before the soldiers come.'

'I'll leave the orders to Gonzalez. Where is Rodriguez?'

'He was not fast enough to shoot the *gringo* captain.' Sanchez shrugged. 'Now I want to see Doctor Lopez before I bleed to death.'

'It will be a waste of time to see the medico. You will be dead the minute Gonzalez sees you.' Emilio motioned to the trail that led into the village. 'Ride in that direction and I will join you when I've fetched my horse.'

Sanchez touched spurs to his mount and went on towards the village. He was not looking forward to facing Gonzalez again. Emilio joined him shortly, and they continued in silence. When they reached the village they dismounted outside the cantina, and Emilio snatched Sanchez's gun from its holster as they approached the doorway.

'It will be safer if you are not armed,' he remarked.

Sanchez looked around quickly when he entered the cantina, and a sigh of relief escaped him when he saw Gonzalez was not present. He limped to the bar and asked for tequila. Martinez served him without comment, and Sanchez could see that the inn keeper was highly nervous. His hand shook when he picked up a bottle, and some tequila spilled on the bar top when he filled the glass. He wiped up the spillage and almost knocked over the glass. Sanchez snatched it up and drank the contents.

'Where is Gonzalez?' Sanchez demanded, speaking with more confidence than he was feeling.

'He's at the medico's getting his shoulder fixed,' Martinez said. 'You are to remain here until he comes back. Where is Rodriguez?'

'The *gringo* captain shot him.' Sanchez moved to a table, sat down to favour his injured leg, and settled himself to await Gonzalez's return. His mind teemed with desperate ideas for escape, but at that moment none seemed realistic enough to be attempted.

'Watch Sanchez closely,' Emilio said, 'and shoot him if he tries to get away. I'll talk to Gonzalez.' He grinned at Sanchez and walked to the door.

Sanchez wiped beads of sweat from his fleshy face and called for another drink. He watched Emilio step out to the street, and was shocked when a gun hammered. Emilio was knocked back by a slug and fell heavily across the doorstep. A shocked silence lasted for split seconds while everyone in the cantina stared at Emilio's body. Then there was a rush for the door, and men pushed outside clutching their guns.

Sanchez remained motionless at the table, wondering if this was a propitious moment to try and escape. His wounded leg was a big disadvantage, and his horse was out front, where the men were gathered. All were talking vociferously about the shooting. Twice Sanchez began to rise, but an innate caution warned him to remain inactive for he would get only one slim chance to escape, and he was afraid of missing it. If he could get clear of the village he could signal to a large group of his men waiting close outside in a defile.

Most of the men came back into the cantina, and minutes later there was a spate of shooting on the street. Sanchez wondered who was getting shot. He wondered if the Yankee soldiers had sneaked across the river to surprise Gonzalez. But when Gonzalez came striding into the cantina, dragging Rosita with him, Sanchez was shocked.

Gonzalez, however, grinned in friendly fashion and came to join Sanchez, holding Rosita by an arm.

'So you have worked out a deal with the *gringos*, no?' Gonzalez said. 'How do we get the guns?'

'They will be handed over to me when you and your men have pulled out of here. But I have to prove that you will not get your hands on the supplies after they are given to me.'

'You would have to kill me to keep that promise, Pedro.' Gonzalez grinned easily, but his eyes glittered wolfishly. 'Is that what you have in mind? Are you thinking of killing your old friend Gonzalez?'

'Your death would serve no purpose,' Sanchez replied. 'I have told you what I'll do. I'll give you the guns when I get them, and then I'll ride away from here. I want nothing more than to continue with my old way of life.'

'Robbing for a few pesos,' Gonzalez sneered. 'The trouble with you, Sanchez, is that you have no ambition. That is what drives a man to improve his lot and make progress.'

'You always had too much ambition,' Sanchez countered sadly.

'Where is Rodriguez?' Gonzalez's expression changed and his lips pinched together.

'He tried to shoot the *gringo* captain but was not fast enough. It was a mistake to send one of your men with me.'

'And you are bleeding. How did that occur?'

'I stopped a stray bullet.' Sanchez shrugged. 'I came back to tell you to pull out of the village or I will not get the supplies, and I must return to the Yankee soldiers shortly. But I have to visit the doctor before I do anything else.'

A shot sounded somewhere outside, and two of Gonzalez's men went out to the street. Tension filled the cantina. Moments later voices were heard outside. Then Gomez appeared in the doorway, followed closely by the Mexican who had captured him. Gonzalez prevented Rosita from running to the man she loved, and she cried out sharply in protest and turned on her father like a wildcat.

'Let me go to him,' she cried. 'He has been hurt.'

Gomez paused on the threshold. He was clutching his right arm just above the elbow, where blood had saturated his shirt. His face was pale and he was in considerable pain, but his expression twisted with hatred for Gonzalez as he gazed at the big man.

'When will you accept that Rosita and I will get married, no matter what you do?' Gomez demanded.

'She cannot marry a dead man.' Gonzalez laughed as he eased his pistol from its holster. The three clicks it made when he cocked the weapon sounded ominous in the sudden silence.

Rosita hurled herself at Gonzalez and seized his right wrist with both hands. The pressure she applied sent a shaft of agony through Gonzalez's wounded shoulder. He cursed and thrust her away so violently she fell in a heap on the floor but then sprang up, ran to Gomez, and threw her arms protectively around him. Gonzalez followed and thrust her away. He lifted his gun and pressed the muzzle against Gomez's right temple.

'I will kill him now if you don't sit down and keep quiet,' Gonzalez rasped. 'Martinez, lock Gomez and my daughter in your store room and I'll deal with them later. Luis, you take Sanchez to the medico, get his leg fixed, and then bring him back. He has a lot more to do today. Sanchez, don't make the mistake of trying to escape. I'll kill you even if it means losing those two wagons.'

Sanchez lurched to the door and one of the Mexicans followed him closely. Martinez escorted Rosita and Gomez to his storeroom and locked them in. Gonzalez struggled against impatience. He sat down at a table, aware, at this moment in time, that all he could do

243

was wait patiently.

'Bring me some food,' he ordered Martinez. 'Later, we'll make another effort to get that wagon out of the river.'

★ ★ ★

Moran conferred with Captain Manning when the wagon that had been on its way to Del Rio returned to the military position on the American side of the river. The grizzled Ranger was keen to move across the border to take the fight to the Mexicans while Moran intimated that he was content to hold his position until reinforcements arrived. Manning shook his head.

'I've been law dealing along this border for more years than I care to remember,' he said, 'and I know these Mexicans better than I know my wife. If half a dozen of us can sneak into that village across the river and get the drop on Gonzalez we'll have them by the tail. Take Gonzalez out and the rest of them will run. So if you and a couple of the soldier boys come along to make up our numbers we can turn this situation without waiting around. Gonzalez had about fifty men when he first came after the wagons yesterday, and I reckon he's called for more and is waiting for them to show up. If we don't make a move right now we'll lose out. This river crossing could be a second Alamo.'

'I'm counting on Sanchez bringing in men to even the odds a little,' Moran said. 'He's got a big stake in this. He wants the guns but he doesn't want a revolution.'

'One of the first things I learned about Mexicans when I started to operate in this area was never to trust one of them.' Manning grimaced as he recalled some of his past exploits.

Moran looked across the river. As far as he could see there wasn't a Mexican within ten miles, but he knew some of them would be watching the stranded wagon. He was tempted to go along with Manning's plan but his orders were clear and he could not disobey them, although he saw the sense in what Manning said. An unexpected attack could relieve the precarious situation in which they were stuck, but, whatever happened, Gonzalez would never get his hands on the guns. One wagon was already rigged with a keg of black powder and a length of fuse wire, and there were enough explosives on the second wagon to destroy it if the need arose. He watched for signs of Sanchez returning, but there was no movement on the far bank.

'I couldn't take any soldiers along,' he mused, returning his attention to Manning. 'It's strictly against army rules for a soldier in uniform to cross the border.'

'Like I said before, you ain't in uniform, and I'd settle for you coming alone if it means going over there and nabbing Gonzalez. There are only four of us Rangers now, and that's slim odds. What do you say, Captain?'

'Nothing is going to happen here

until sundown,' Moran observed, 'and I'm getting mighty impatient lying here just twiddling my thumbs.' He glanced around, saw Lieutenant Anderson nearby, and called him over. 'Lieutenant, I'm thinking of taking a ride across the river with the Rangers to try and grab Gonzalez. You can hold on here until I get back, huh?'

'I reckon, Captain. There'll be no more attacks unless Gonzalez gets help.'

'Are you clear on my orders to destroy that wagon if it looks like being recaptured by Gonzalez?' Moran persisted.

'No sweat,' Lieutenant Anderson nodded. 'I've posted a man under it with specific orders, and there's enough explosives to blow the wagon and its contents into tiny pieces and spread them over half of Mexico. As soon as it's dark, we'll rig up the stranded wagon likewise.'

'I hope to be back before sundown,' Moran mused. He glanced at Manning. 'OK. I'll go along with you, Captain.'

Manning grinned. 'I thought you'd never agree, so let's get at them. I've been in that village several times and know it well. If Gonzalez is holed up there then I'm confident we can grab him. It ain't strictly according to the law, but I have been known to work purely from a justice angle, and at the moment it sure looks like Gonzalez should be taken out, legally or otherwise. There's a price on his head over here, and if we can take him alive we'll bring him back, put him on trial, and both justice and the law will be properly served. Let's get moving. The sooner we make our play the better.'

They fetched their horses and mounted up. Moran feared he was making a mistake, but he was willing to try anything that would enable him to obey his orders. He was happy for Captain Manning to take command, and they rode upstream for at least a mile before crossing the river into Mexico. Manning proved that he knew what he was doing. He led his little band on a circuitous route in order to approach the village from the south. When they were within sight of the community they rode into cover and edged forward until they were close enough to dismount and lead their horses the rest of the way on foot.

'All we wanta do is take Gonzalez and bundle him back across to our side of the border,' Manning said as they picketed their mounts at the side of a building on the edge of the village. 'We'll stick close together and head across the back lots to the cantina. That's the focal point around here, and I reckon that's where we'll find Gonzalez, if he's still around. Let's try and do this without shooting. If we do get hold of Gonzalez then his men won't give us any trouble. They'll break and run like the rats they are. Anyway, from what I've heard, the folks in this village are for Sanchez, not Gonzalez.'

Moran nodded, and they checked their weapons before sneaking forward along the rear of the buildings fronting the street.

Sanchez was escorted to the doctor's house to receive treatment for his leg wound. Doctor Lopez, a keen Sanchez supporter and one of Gonzalez's most dedicated enemies, insisted on treating Sanchez in his office without his armed escort, and the man remained outside the door. While they were alone in the office, Lopez offered Sanchez his full support.

'I don't want you to become involved against Gonzalez,' Sanchez said. 'You are too valuable to this community to risk your life for me. Just give me a gun and I will kill Gonzalez. I have decided that it is the only way to stop him.'

'You can have as many guns as you want,' Lopez said. 'But I don't think you can kill Gonzalez without help.'

'I have to make the attempt,' Sanchez replied heavily.

Lopez opened a drawer, took out a pistol and handed it over. Sanchez checked the weapon and sat clutching it while the doctor finished treating his leg wound. When he was ready to leave he arose and tested his leg, grimacing at the pain he felt when he put his full weight on it. He opened the door of the office and his escort, who was standing at a window overlooking the street, turned, saw the levelled gun Sanchez was holding, and raised his hands without hesitation.

'Lock him in my store room,' Lopez said.

Sanchez did so, and then stuffed the man's pistol in his waistband. He took his leave by the doctor's back door and made his way along the back lots, heading for the alley opposite the cantina. There he paused, watching the street and considering his options.

Gonzalez sat eating a meal in the cantina, with Martinez standing in close attendance. When Gonzalez finished eating, Martinez cleared his throat.

'Shall I give your daughter some food?' he asked.

Gonzalez considered for a moment

before nodding. 'Feed her and Gomez. I may not kill Gomez until later. Bring me a cigar, Martinez.'

The inn-keeper attended to Gonzalez's wants and then ordered his wife to fill two plates with food. He led the way to the store room, and stood on guard with a pistol in his hand while his wife entered. Rosita spurned the meal but Gomez had better sense and accepted it. He approached the door to confront Martinez.

'You are not Gonzalez's man,' Gomez said. 'Why do you obey him?'

'To stay alive,' Martinez replied, and grinned. He motioned for his wife to leave, and waited until she was out of earshot before handing his pistol to Gomez. 'I'll not lock this door,' he said sibilantly. 'Give me time to get back into the cantina before you leave. Go out the back door and make a run for it. If you stay here you will be dead before tomorrow's sunrise.'

Gomez was astonished, but grinned as he checked the loads in the pistol.

He thrust the weapon into his holster, turned his attention to the laden plate, and began to eat voraciously, pausing only to advise Rosita to do the same.

'I do not want you to kill my father,' Rosita said. 'Promise me.'

'I won't unless I have to do it to save my own life,' Gomez replied. 'Now eat. We don't know when we'll get the chance of another meal.'

Rosita nibbled at the food. Gonzalez finished his quickly, pushed the plate aside, and drew the gun.

'Come on,' he said urgently. 'It is time to leave.'

He went to the door, opened it carefully and peered out. He could hear the mumble of voices coming from the big public room, and recognized Gonzalez's voice as the bullying Mexican nagged Martinez. For an interminable moment Gomez stood motionless while he considered killing Gonzalez. But Rosita pushed him urgently in the back and the impulse left him. He ushered Rosita to the back door and opened it quietly. When he looked out across the back lots he saw no one. Silence and heat were oppressive.

He made Rosita follow him, and went along the rear of the buildings to the edge of the village. When he rounded the corner of the end house he pulled up short, for there were horses standing with trailing reins, and half a dozen men were motionless with guns in their hands. Gomez began to lift his gun but it was quickly snatched out of his hand, and then he recognized Moran and saw Ranger badges on the chests of the other four men.

'Where did you two come from?' Moran demanded.

'What are you doing on this side of the border, Captain?' Rosita countered. Her tense face changed expression as she guessed at the reason for their presence. 'You've come to kill my father!' she gasped.

'Only if he resists,' Captain Manning said firmly. 'Is Gonzalez in the cantina?'

'No,' Rosita said quickly.

'Yes,' Gomez contradicted sharply.

'You'd better get away from here,' Moran addressed Rosita. 'Go back to your aunt's ranch. You should be safe there. I'll come and talk to you when this business is settled. If we can, we'll take your father alive.'

Gomez took hold of Rosita's arm and began to drag her away. She pulled against him.

'We'll pick up our horses and leave,' he said, 'and you'll come with me without struggling if you want me to stay away from Gonzalez.'

Rosita stopped struggling and walked ahead of Gomez towards the street.

'Let's get moving,' Manning said. 'We'll go along the rear of the buildings and get into the cantina by the back door.'

'You know the way,' Moran told him, and Manning took the lead, his gun ready in his hand.

Moran followed closely. The three Rangers moved in behind him. When they reached the cantina, Manning did not pause. He opened the door and entered quickly. Moran held his gun ready for action. Señora Martinez was busy in the kitchen. She looked up at them and then returned to her cooking as if she was accustomed to armed strangers passing through her kitchen. Manning touched a finger to the brim of his hat as his gaze met her eyes. Her expression did not change, and he continued to the big public room.

Manning did not hesitate. He pushed open the door, strode into the bar, and moved quickly to his right to clear the doorway. Moran stepped in beside him, He saw Gonzalez lounging at a small table, smoking a cigar. There were seven other Mexicans in the room, seated and at ease; Martinez was standing behind the bar, wiping glasses, his face showing despair. He was sweating profusely. Martinez caught the movement of the Rangers as they entered silently and turned his head to look at them, his eyes widening. He raised his hands immediately. At that moment Sanchez appeared in the street doorway on the far side of Gonzalez. He was holding his gun. Gonzalez, distracted by Sanchez, half rose from his seat and reached impulsively for his pistol.

'Go ahead,' Sanchez said. 'I am looking for a reason to kill you, Gonzalez.'

Gonzalez jerked his hands away from his waist.

One of the men seated at the other tables slid a hand beneath the table top. Sanchez flicked the muzzle of his pistol in the man's direction and fired a shot. The bullet slammed through the top of the table and struck the Mexican in the stomach. His screech of pain cut through the crash of the shot. He jerked upright and then fell heavily to the floor.

'Don't shoot Sanchez,' Moran rapped sharply to his companions, and the sound of his voice cut incisively through the fading gunshot.

Gonzalez glanced over his shoulder, saw the Rangers and recognized Moran. Despite the fact that he was covered by Sanchez's gun, Gonzalez hurled himself to the floor and drew his pistol as his table overturned. His movement galvanized his men at the other tables into action. They jumped up, pulled their guns, and started shooting.

Sanchez triggered his pistol. His eyes were expressionless. Sweat was running down his face. He saw Gonzalez clear leather and swing the deadly muzzle of his gun in his direction. Aware of Gonzalez's speed, Sanchez's first shot was hurried, and his bullet struck the table top behind which Gonzalez had ducked. The slug passed through the thin wood and struck Gonzalez in the left elbow. Sanchez grew desperate and fired again. All he could see of Gonzalez was his sombrero, and he tried to put his slugs through the crown.

Moran turned his gun loose on the other Mexicans, who were diving from their seats. He beat the nearest man to the shot and saw him throw his arms wide before slumping to the floor. The Rangers were already in action, cool and unhurried, their aim deadly in the close confines of the big room. Their pistols boomed and the remaining Mexicans went down like corn being scythed. Gun echoes blasted rapidly, shaking the dusty bottles on the shelves behind the bar, where Martinez had thrown himself to the floor as the first shot was fired.

Gonzalez snapped off a shot at Sanchez. The bullet thudded into Sanchez's left shoulder. Sanchez staggered but did not go down. His mouth gaped and he gasped for breath. He thumbed back his hammer and set himself to hit Gonzalez dead centre. He fired, and his shot rang out as Gonzalez squeezed his trigger. Moran saw Gonzalez jerk. The Mexican came up off the floor, spun around, and then pitched down out of sight, squeezing his trigger spasmodically as he took Sanchez's second bullet through his heart.

Sanchez stood motionless, his feet planted solidly on the floor, anchored by his great weight. Blood showed on his left shoulder, but for a seemingly endless moment his body remained erect before he fell forward on to his face with a force that shook the cantina.

The big room filled quickly with drifting gun smoke, thick and pungent, but the shooting dwindled away as the Mexicans fell to the flaming guns of law and order.

The gun echoes faded. Moran glanced around. One of the Rangers, Wade, had dropped his gun and was clasping his left arm from which blood was seeping. He grinned at Moran and bent to retrieve his fallen gun. Moran went forward to check Gonzalez. He found the big man stretched out on his back, arms flung wide, his vacant gaze fixed in a sightless stare at the gloomy ceiling. Moran went on to where Sanchez was lying on the threshold, and to his relief he found the big man alive, bleeding from a shoulder wound.

Martinez emerged from behind the bar. Moran turned to him.

'Fetch the doctor over here,' he ordered.

'Maria,' Martinez called. 'Go get the doctor.'

Señora Martinez came hurrying through the public room, stepping over sprawled bodies, and went to the street door, not looking left or right. She departed silently. Manning, who had taken the time to reload the empty chambers in his pistol, suddenly stiffened and hurried to the nearest window overlooking the street. He peered out.

'Riders coming,' he announced. 'About twenty of them, all loaded for bear.'

Moran started for the door but Sanchez called to him.

'They will be my men, Captain,' he said. 'I had them standing by outside the village, and signalled to them to come in as I came in here to kill Gonzalez. We will take those wagons off your hands now.'

'I shall be glad to see the back of them,' Moran said.

'Help me up,' Sanchez commanded. 'I must show myself to my men.'

Moran helped Sanchez to his feet and they went out to the street. Sanchez waved and the newcomers came up and dismounted. Moran heaved a long sigh of relief as Sanchez's weight was taken from his supporting arm by a couple of the Mexicans. It came to him that at last the fight was at an end. Captain Manning emerged from the cantina followed by his Rangers, and Moran joined them as they went for their horses. He paused beside Sanchez.

'We'll get that stranded wagon out of the river now,' he said. 'You can come and pick up the supplies when you're ready. They'll be waiting for you.'

Sanchez nodded, and the relief showing in his eyes was shared by Moran as he went with the Rangers.

THE END

We do hope that you have enjoyed reading this large print book.

Did you know that all of our titles are available for purchase?

We publish a wide range of high quality large print books including:
Romances, Mysteries, Classics
General Fiction
Non Fiction and Westerns

Special interest titles available in large print are:
The Little Oxford Dictionary
Music Book, Song Book
Hymn Book, Service Book

Also available from us courtesy of Oxford University Press:
Young Readers' Dictionary
(large print edition)
Young Readers' Thesaurus
(large print edition)

For further information or a free brochure, please contact us at:
Ulverscroft Large Print Books Ltd.,
The Green, Bradgate Road, Anstey,
Leicester, LE7 7FU, England.
Tel: (00 44) 0116 236 4325
Fax: (00 44) 0116 234 0205

Other titles in the
Linford Western Library:

APPLEJACK

Emmett Stone

When old-timer Applejack disappears after claiming to have struck it rich, Marshal Rupe Cooley has more important things to take care of, like dealing with the vicious outlaw Cage Drugget. When Applejack is recognized carrying out a bank robbery with Drugget's gang, Cooley saddles up and sets out after them. Meeting more of Drugget's victims along the way, his resolve to bring the gang boss down intensifies. Will he find the hideout in time? And what is the truth about Applejack's fortune?

FORTRESS PALOMINO

Michael D. George

As the grasslands of War Smoke fill with steers for the coming trail drives, Marshal Matt Fallen wires other lawmen for help in keeping his town peaceful until the drift moves north. Kid Palomino and his sidekick, Red Rivers, heed the call and ride in to help. When they discover that notorious bandit Santiago Del Rosa has crossed the border with his gang, they don't hesitate to leap into action. Can Kid and Rivers stop Santiago before more blood is spilled?

TWILIGHT TRAIL

Lance Howard

When manhunter Teel Barsom brings in notorious outlaw Slade Heath he makes a fateful mistake, destroying the new life he's built with his young bride and riddling his nightmares with guilt and loss. Trapped in a world of whiskey and shame, Teel wants nothing more than to sink into despair when a mysterious young woman abducts him from the saloon and offers him redemption. But with salvation comes a price, one that may cost him and his kidnapper their lives . . .